THE SUPPLICANT

A Novel by RONALD HAAK

"And there was a great battle in heaven, Michael and his angels fought with the dragon, and the dragon fought and his angels: And they prevailed not, neither was their place found anymore in heaven. And that great dragon was cast out, that old serpent, who is called the devil and Satan, who seduceth the whole world; and he was cast unto the earth, and his angels were thrown down with him."

Apocalypse 12: 7 - 9

THE SUPPLICANT

CHAPTER 1

A darkening cloud filled sky, hovers over an old, ornately sculptured black, faded, and rusting wrought iron gate, blocking the entrance, to a leafless tree lined road, leading the way to the, Northeastern Pennsylvania Hospital for the Criminally Insane. A massively structured aging brick, and stone constructed grey slate, and gabled building, ominously awaiting visitors at the end of the road, as dead leaves blow wildly across the road ahead, filling the air with a foreboding dread of what awaits them.

In a darkened room inside this archaic institution, a man is lying on the psychiatrist's couch, facing away from the doctor. Dr. Black's left hand rests on his left knee, holding a note book, his legs are crossed. He is writing something in the bottom of the note book's page, which is full of notations, with the point of an ornately designed, opulent pen, the writers right hand is unseen.

The man, Homicide Detective John (Jack) Ramsey is dressed in a hospital gown, robe, slippers, and has an orange plastic I.D. band on his left wrist. He is smoking a worn down, long ash tipped cigarette in his right hand as he talks. In his left hand he is holding an ash tray, which he is balancing on his stomach. Jack's hands shake as he speaks, smoking incessantly, gesturing with his right hand as he talks, as the long grey ash from his cigarette falls onto many others lying on his ash strewn hospital gown.

He seems to shake throughout his whole body, stammering slightly, as he talks. He is obviously weak, fearful of the future, knowing in his very soul that there is no way out, speaking slowly, as though it is painful for him to speak.

"It all started ... after my wife," covering his face, trying to compose himself, as best he can before continuing. "After my wife and daughter, well they were never found. I ...

... I lost my mind I guess. All I could think of was finding that bastard, finding the bastard and finding out where my wife and daughter were. I found my daughter's rag doll, which she would never, never willingly leave, behind ..."

Jack turns to look at the psychiatrist at this point. His eyes, dark circles of pain, then he lays back down again.

"... she took that doll everywhere. I clung to that doll, Janie was her name, I ..." Jack continues to recount the story of his missing wife and daughter. "I started to retrace my steps leading back to the trail which lead me to this ..." At this point Jack's voice trails off, and we are taken back in time ...

... Into a pitch black, dimly lit bedroom, as a very powerfully strong looking Jack, lovingly watches his sleeping wife Diane. His joy is obviously apparent, as he quietly leans over her curvaceous body, covering her with her blankets, and kisses her lovely face. He then smiles a quiet contented smile, and exits their bedroom. Jack is buttoning up his dress shirt, and slipping on his dapper pin striped suit jacket as he walks, down the dimly lit hallway.

Stopping to look in on his sleeping daughter Nicole, as he always does, every morning before he leaves for work. Her stuffed animals watching over her, as she happily dreams of sugar plums, while clutching her rag doll Janie to her heart, smiling as she sleeps in her cozy toy filled bedroom. Jack lingers a long time, happily watching his little child sleeping, and after many enjoyable moments silently spent watching her, he quietly enters her bedroom, tiptoes to her bedside, and leaning over her sleeping body, kisses his little Nicole on the forehead.

Reentering the hallway, while still watching her sleep, and after a happy moment of quiet reflection, he closes her door ever so quietly, and resumes walking down the hallway, then down the stairs, grabs his leather jacket, walks to the front door, and exits into the street.

As dawn's first light is trying to break above the sky line off in the distance, Jack leaves his home for work, never to see his lovely wife Diane, or his little child Nicole ever again.

CHAPTER 2

Jack skips forward in his story, to a more recent time, when he was still trying to deal with the loss of his family. Having never found them, but still hoping they will turn up. He struggled every day, trying to deal with his now empty life, and his deeply troubling job. As the skeletal remains of very young children and their mothers were being discovered, Jack found it all too painfully close to home.

As Jack continues to relate his past to Dr. Black … the light in the dimly lit hospital room fades to black as Jack quietly speaks of the past …

"… I remember it was unusually cold one early morning, in October as I drove along a lonely wooded moon lit road, beside a river. Rain drops hitting the car's roof and the sound of the windshield wipers, as they moved across the windshield …"

… as we slip back in time….

… We see Jack's big black car is traveling northwest on the East River Drive. A small red light, on top of the dashboard, flashes slowly, while the headlights and red lights hidden in the car's front grill, alternately flash on and off quickly, as the car goes through a broken red light at a flooded intersection.

"it always seemed to go from summer straight into winter, with no fall in between …"

As the sound of the wind howls, and Fairmount Park's trees blow about to the right and left, Jack's car comes into view, and continues on out of sight along the lonely road. The rain is turning into a mixture of sleet and rain, on the windshield, as Jack drives through the park.

"It had been a little over a year since my families disappearance. Since then three children's skeletal remains had been found in Fairmount Park, this will make the fourth." We see his eyes looking into the rear view mirror, "in the beginning, I thought I would just wake up, and this would all be but a dream, but it didn't ..."

"... but I can't go home, and I couldn't give up, and sell the house. I kept thinking they'll just come home one day, so I kept it, but I can't go there, can't live there, too many ghosts. So I live in a rooming house, above a bar, but now I find myself waking up in strange places, and not knowing how I got there, or why I was there."

Two Philadelphia Police Officers calmly talk to each other, while standing at their positions, beside their cars, and the other array of police and emergency vehicles…. An ambulance driver speaks to a police officer, as they start to smoke cigarettes from a pack the driver has offered…. The open rear doors of the ambulance reveal an empty stretcher inside, while police tape cordons off the area behind the police cars, leading back into the woods.

Jack's big black car is now speeding along a winding dirt road, as a small stream meanders along on the left. He climbs up a slight hill, as he goes deeper into the woods. A light rain sleet mix continues to fall, in the darkness of the night, onto the windshield as police cruiser's flashing lights begin to appear off in the distance.

As Jack's mind wanders into the depths of the past ... "There's lights back in the woods, flashing lights back in the woods. Police car's headlights back in the woods, there's death back in the woods." Jack whispers to himself, while slowly drinking a can of beer as he drives.

Jack finishes the can of beer just before he pulls up to the crime scene. Before he gets out, he crumples up the can, and hides it in a paper bag, on the floor along with the others, and tucks the bag under the seat of the car. He looks into the rear view mirror.

Jack's eyes, sleepless sockets of pain are looking back. He wets his fingers with his tongue, and rubs his eyes. Looking as though he was expecting someone to talk to him … and then, after a time, he abandons his thoughts, and exits the car, spraying a breath freshener into his mouth as he does so.

It is barely raining now, but still mixed with sleet, as Jack wearily gets out, and puts on an old chocolate colored leather jacket. He turns up the weathered collar, buttons up a few buttons, and pulls on a black wool cap. He then grabs a flash light, puts it in his jacket pocket, ducks under the yellow crime scene tape, and walks toward the lights. A police dog, and his handler are at work off in the distance, as he walks down the hill, and approaches a police officer coming up.

Jack speaks to the police officer, "Hi Bill, what do we have?"

"It's two bodies, one's a child, Doc's look's at 'em now," motioning off into the woods, "they're over here Lieutenant."

As they walk through the woods, the policeman takes out a pack of cigarettes, and offers one to Jack. "Like a smoke Lieutenant."

"No thanks Bill, I'm trying to quit," looking down, as he is turning his plain gold wedding ring, with the fingers of his other hand, "I promised someone I would." Bill taps the pack against his hand, takes one out, and lights it up. As Jack follows the policeman down into the woods.

"There's the child Lieutenant." The policeman points to where the body lies, and then returns to walking back up the hill. In the near distance a morose, overweight, coroner is examining something in a depression dug into the earth.

As a somber and deep in thought Jack approaches, the doctor is taking off his examination gloves, and looking down into the shallow earthen grave.

"Hi Doc."

Doc looks up, and seeing Jack smiles. "Well, here we go again Jack."

Jack nods his head, as he peers down into the earthen grave, and sees the contents, "Yeah, I know." Kneeling down, Jack shines his flashlight into the grave, but extreme anxiety overwhelms Jack at this point, because he never knows if this is the body of his little child Nicole.

The little child's battered, decomposing body, is barely visible now, because Jack's flashlight beam has trailed off the child, and now shines into the woods behind him, as his head drops on to his chest, and he tries to compose himself.

Jack's face reveals that he is trying not to cry, but tears start to run down his cheeks, as a kindly and compassionate Doc speaks understandingly.

"Where's that inquisitive mind Jack?"

Jack seemingly doesn't hear Doc's question. His thoughts are off somewhere, as he continues staring down into the shallow grave. The Doc is looking around as he approaches Jack, and speaking quietly.

"Jack?" speaking a little louder, he again says.

"Jack," as the Doc gently places his hand on Jack's shoulder, a startled Jack stands up, looks at the Doc for a second, and then turns and looks back at the child.

"Oh, I guess I was off somewhere else."

Doc kindly laughs to himself, and smiles at Jack, as he takes a gnawed unlit cigar from his mouth. Smiling playfully, but inside he is sad for his friend Jack.

"I said, where's that inquisitive mind of yours Jack?"

Jack shrugs his shoulders, and continues to look down at the remains of the child.

"I don't know Doc."

As Doc tries to relight his cigar, he turns to the child's grave, looks again at her, and then back to Jack. Puffing on his cigar now, pausing as he's leaving, "Call me tomorrow, I'll have the results of the autopsy by then, late in the afternoon, all right Jack?" Doc then picks up his medical bag, and starts to go, but stops.

"Call me then, but I'll tell you this, something's chewed on her."

Jack seems to tremble slightly, and the Doc pats Jack's back gently.

"Sure you're in the right business Jack?"

Jack shrugs his shoulders, without taking his eyes off the child. Doc looks around at the other uniformed police who are looking into the woods with their flash lights, off in the distance, their backs being barely visible. Doc looks around, puts his medical bag back down, takes out a flask from within his coats inner pocket, unscrews the cap and offers Jack a drink. Jack bangs back a healthy jolt, and hands it back. The Doc takes one too, and puts the flask away. Jack watches his good friend.

"Thanks Doc."

Doc gently pats Jack's back, as he starts to leave. "I'll tell the boys they can take her, when your through. See ya tomorrow Jack."

Jack nods to the Doc, and watches him pick up his medical bag, and walk off up the hill. He then returns his gaze to the little child, and holds his head, then walks off to the side, and stands there watching nothing, as he thinks about the past.

More police officers arrive, bringing lights of all description, some police are in white outfits, they stake out the area with yellow tape. Jack moves further away and watches them, thinking to himself ...

"There was nothing to be done here until it got light.... In my mind, I imagined I went home and looked in on my little girl. She was only about four and a half then, sleeping with Janie, her rag doll, beside her pillow. ... I felt like I was going to be sick. I started way too late to raise a family, an I knew it." Sleet continues to fall, covering Jack's jacket, and wool capped head.

That afternoon, as the sun hovers over the heavily wooded tree line, an exhausted Jack walks slowly up the hill toward his car, tired, wet, and cold. All but a few police cars remain on the scene now, the other vehicles long gone. He opens the door, gets in, and then drives off back down the dirt road till he hits the river, then turns on to the East River Drive.

Jack drives along the East River Drive, heading back towards the Art Museum. He turns on to the cross town expressway, and heads east through center city Philly. Exiting the expressway, he then drives though Sharktown, turns on to Front Street, and drives north under the cover of the elevated train tracks.

CHAPTER 3

Soon after entering Fishtown, Jack pulls up next to a no parking sign, and gets out. Walks across the street, walks up the steps, under an old weathered sign which reads PETE'S PLACE, and enters through the front door, beside an old and peeling sign that reads Fine Food & Drink. Then through a set of swinging doors, and walks in to an empty, whiskey smelling bar. An old dog gets up from the saw dust covered old wooden floor, and approaches Jack to smell his leg, and say hello, as Jack lovingly rubs Bruno's head.

There are a few impoverished old men at one end of the bar drinking draft beers and cheap muscatel, talking in murmured voices. Jack approaches the bar, removes his coat, places it on the back of a stool, puts a twenty on the bar, and sits down. A large tattooed armed bartender appears to wake up, as he puts down his Daily News, and walks toward him, looking at his watch as he is shaking his head back and forth, and smiling at Jack in a playful sort of way, feigning moral judgement.

A smiling Jack says, "I know, I know, come on Pete, I'm not a camel," waving him closer, "I'm thirsty, get yourself one."

"Okay, okay, I was only kiddin', come on Jack relax."

Pete pours out a double of Irish whiskey, draws a pint of Budweiser, and sets them down in front of Jack, then he pours himself a whiskey.

Jack raises his whiskey in a toast. "Nostrovia." Then they drink, and Pete fills them up again. The drinks seem to disappear. Jack lifts his empty beer glass, and gestures to Pete to fill it up again.

"Boy, your gettin' slow Pete."

"Okay, okay I guess I deserve it, this next round is on me."

Pete refills Jack's drinks, and then refills his own.

Later that afternoon, a visibly tired looking Jack gets up from the bar stool, and grabs his jacket off the back of the seat. An as he drinks the last of his beer, he gropes in his pockets for some money, and motions for Pete, whose reading his newspaper.

"I better get some sleep, I've got to go back in pretty soon. Give me a six pack, an a bottle Pete. Okay?"

Pete talks as he puts a six pack of beer, and some ice, into a doubled paper bag.

"Now you know I can't do that, although I'd like to help you out," he makes a face, "but I can't, I'd like to, but I can't, it's against the law to sell a bottle of whiskey across the bar ..."

He then takes an unopened bottle of Irish whisky from the bars liquor shelf, puts it into another paper bag, and sets them both on the bar, in front of Jack.

" ... but, I can lend you one."

"Thanks Pete."

Jack lifts his whiskey glass, nods his head in gratitude, and finishes his whiskey. He then leaves the money on the bar, picks up the bags, walks to, and opens a side door, revealing a banister'd stairway leading up into the bars rooming house.

As Pete watches him leave, his smile turns to a sad frown, and slowly shakes his head in sympathy for Jack, as he picks up the money.

"Take care Jack," under his breath, "take care."

Jack walks through the doorway leading to the staircase, and is seen climbing the steps. The sound of a beer can top pops, as Jack slowly disappears up the steps.

Jack walks up another flight of steps, and after yet another flight, he steps on to the landing. Jack walks down the long hallway, at the end of which there is a large double hung wooden window facing out onto the street, and with the aid of his keys, he enters his room. As the sound of a beer can hitting the floor is heard. Jack slurs out ...

... "Damn it" as the door behind him closes quietly.

Jack's small dark room consists of a bureau, desk, chair, twin steel spoke framed bed, and a small lamp on top of a night stand. All of which are clean, but very old. His room also has a large window beside the bed, which looks out on to the side street below. On Jack's night stand, beside the lamp sits an old radio, small glowing dialed electric clock and a framed picture of a young looking woman and a very small child, smiling joyfully, holding her Janie from some happier time in the past.

The room is black, except for the light filtering in from the street light out on the corner. As Jack wakes up he fumbles around in the dark looking for something to drink, finds a beer in a paper bag under the bed, sits back down on the bed, and drinks in the dark, staring back into the past.

As Janie watches, from a corner of the small blackened room, a drunken Jack is quietly loading a snub nosed 38 revolver, expertly, methodically, and very purposefully.

Later that night Jack walks lethargically down the street, drinking the remains of the bottle of whiskey. He stops at a boarded up row house's steps, up the block from Pete's, and sits down mumbling quietly, talking to himself as he drinks.

CHAPTER 4

The next morning uniformed police officers are standing outside of the police precinct, out on the sidewalk in small groups, casually talking to each other. While a line of several patrol cars are angle parked, out in the street in front of them. As a tired, half shaven, wrinkled suited Jack, walks past the police officers out on the sidewalk, and up the steps of the station house. After he passes them, the police officers look in his direction, and then back to each other, as a cruel looking smile forms on their faces, and after Jack enters the building, they laugh among themselves, gesturing toward Jacks retreating direction.

Jack lumbers up the stairs, past other uniformed police officers coming down. The police officers look at Jack after he is past, whisper to each other, and then laugh quietly. Jack looks ever so slightly towards the laughter, then continues on up the staircase, and down the hallway. He then opens a door marked Homicide Division, on the obscure glass, in faded gold leafed lettering, and goes in.

Jack walks past rows of neat desks, containing folders, papers, trays of forms, phones, lying on top of the desk's in a haphazard, but orderly working manner. Detectives, and uniformed police officers sit, stand, and walk or talk on phones or to themselves, scattered around the room in apparent organized chaos.

Jack stops at a desk, which is a mess of stacks of folders, papers, over flowing paper trays, and old coffee cups. He sits down, and after searching through the cluttered drawers, takes out a bottle of aspirins. He takes out four or five, takes them and then looks about for something to drink. Then gets up and walks to the water cooler, tries to get some water, and finds out that it is empty. There is no water in the bottle, throwing up his arms slightly, giving up he swallow them.

Some of the other detective's huddle together, and laugh about something, sneaking looks in Jacks direction. One of them, a weaselly looking Detective Johnson approaches Jack.

"Hey Jack." Jack stops what he is doing as Detective Johnson comes over. Detective Johnson turns, and winks to his friends, a sly smile on his cruel face. "So what's up Jack? Hey you've got a bit of something here, on your sleeve. You don't want that there now do you Jack?"

Jack looks at his jacket's sleeve, absentmindedly.

"What?"

While Detective Johnson laughingly looks to his pals, who are inching closer.

"Jack, what's this here on your sleeve?" Detective Johnson brushes at Jack's sleeve with his hand. He then straightens Jack's tie as he talks. A smiling Detective Johnson looks back at his pals now, and winks.

"There you go Jack, now you look like something."

Jack looks at their laughing faces, now understanding what is going on. Jack looks with a cold deadly stare right at Detective Johnson. A frightened Johnson backs away from Jack, and lowers his gaze, he is not laughing now. As a ferocious looking Jack looks back at the other detectives, they have all scattered, already walking away in different directions, and when he looks back at Johnson he is gone too.

Later Jack is sitting at his desk, looking at his notes, lost in his thoughts. As a much younger neatly attired black detective, Jack's superior officer, Captain Joseph Shaw watches him a few moments, noticing his unshaven appearance, and shakes his head. He then walks towards his glass walled office, stops at his door, and looks back at Jack ... "Jack! Get the hell in here."

Jack gathers his stuff up on the desk, covers it up, puts some of it in his top drawer, locks it, and walks into the Captains office. Captain Shaw is taking off his suit jacket, he hangs it on a clothes tree against the wall, and sits down. Staring furiously at Jack with an attitude.

"Jack you've been putting in too many hours, and getting nowhere! Now, sit down." Jack sits down in the open chair in front of the desk, looking about restlessly, trying to contain his rage.

Shaw sarcastically glares at Jack. "Things have changed since you started being a cop. Life's changed, attitudes, importance. Are you getting my drift Jack! But, you've stayed the same, and we need change, now think about that, and get the hell out, and clean up your act."

As Jack watches the Captain, a ferocious hatred of him over comes him.

The Captain's eyes suddenly drop, before Jack's intense gaze, and he pretends to study his paper work.

Jack who looks like he is about to kill Shaw, storms out of the room, without closing the door, grabs his jacket off the back of his chair, and walks off, toward the Homicide Divisions door, and exits.

CHAPTER 5

Jack is walking along the sidewalk, beside a chain link fence, leading from a fenced in parking lot. As the wind blows multi colored leaves down the street, an old piece of newspaper wraps around Jacks pants leg, it was blowing along with the leaves. Jack dislodges it, and continues on his way. He is walking slowly, thinking quietly as he walks. He still has not shaved, and his clothes are more wrinkled than before. He walks up the steps, beside the loading dock, enters the back door of the city morgue, and finds himself at a locked security glass door.

Jack waves to the policeman, who is behind a glass wall, seated at a desk, watching the security screens, and holding the daily news open in his hands. A half-eaten hoagie, sits in its wrappings on the desk. The policeman pushes a button to let Jack in. The sound of a buzzer is heard, as Jack opens the door, and enters the buildings hallway.

"It's going to be a long night Lieutenant."

"I hope not."

The two share a laugh, as he walks past the policeman, and down the hallway. Jack continues down the long hallway, all the way to the end, straight into a waiting elevator car, and walks out of sight, moments later the doors close.

The elevator doors open onto almost total darkness, but for a few low hanging round metal lamps, casting small circles of light onto the dark corridor's floor.

As Jack exits the elevator, into the darkness of the long hallway, he passes under a small circle of light and is then thrown back into the darkness. This happens again, and again, as the blackened hallway leads a hesitant Jack towards the morgue's operating theater.

At the end of the sanitized green tiled hallway, he pushes open one of a pair of extra wide, swinging stainless steel doors. Jack is holding one of the doors open as he looks, fifty feet past the empty metal gurneys, at the last murdered child's decomposed body. Doc is performing an autopsy, speaking into a microphone hanging from the ceiling, as he works. Only muffled sounds are heard, like someone mumbling.

Jack cannot watch, backing out of the doorway, he walks to, and sits down on a long wooden bench, in another long dark hallway shooting out to the right, and waits for the doctor to finish. Jack takes out a beer can from his jacket pocket, and coughs, as he pops the top. Leaning back against the sanitized pale green tiled walls, he takes a long drink, then another and after a time ...

… as a weary Jack leans against the wall, he drifts off, and falls asleep....

... he is moving around like he is seeing something, while mumbling something, and his eyes are moving under the lids....

... Jack is dreaming, of a beautiful garden, but it is in a mist like a fog, and it is a black fog, not gray like it should be. The dreams in black and white, and it is cold, cold as ice.

The flowers in the garden are grouped into bunches, lined up into rows like a cemetery's row of graves. As Jack walks along the rows, he is picking flowers, one from each group, and their dripping

30

something dark from where they were picked, and it is on his hands, dark red, It is …

… blood, and the blood is running down Jack's arms, dripping from his elbows on to the ground, as he is walking through this strange looking garden.

At the end of the row of flowers is an open grave, waiting for someone, but now somehow the picked flowers have changed into a bloody looking black and blue little doll, and the doll has become Nicole's Janie.…

A very somber looking, tear filled Jack, kneels down and places little Janie into her waiting grave. Wiping away tears with the back of his hand, as he is slowly covering her body, from a pile of dark soil beside her grave, and he is crying heavily.…

... While from somewhere off in the fog, Jack hears a quiet voice calling to him ...

"Jack ... Jack are you all right?"

... Powerful hands are now gently shaking Jack ...

... "Jack ... Jack ..." Jack sees the Doc hovering over him, but like through a fog, when he awakens from his dream.

"Huh ... oh," looking around sleepily, "what ... what is it Doc?"

Jack is still holding on to the half empty beer can with one hand, and as he sits up straight, he rubs his eyes with his hands, spilling some of the remaining beer onto himself as he does so.

A compassionate, and kindly looking Doc, gently rubs Jack's back, as he speaks. "Come on Jack, let's get us some coffee. There's a machine over here, it doesn't taste very good, but it's hot." Doc's chewing on an unlit cigar, as he helps Jack up on to his feet.

31

The two of them walk off down the long dark corridor, beneath the occasional low round metal lamps hanging from the high dark ceiling. Going in and out of the prolonged darkness as they walk.

"You know Jack, you and me should go fish'n, out in the ocean on my boat, sometime, she's a beauty thirty-two footer ..." Relighting his cigar, as he walks. "God now that's livin."

Jack takes out another beer can from his chocolate colored leather jacket pocket. The sound of a beer can top pops, as he opens the tab, and quietly drinks it while they walk. Doc rubs Jack's back a little as they go into the darkness again.

Doc is watching Jack, and kindly smiling, as he talks. "The kind of life I love. Always have, just you and the sea. There's a kind of purity in that." Doc's puffing happily now, on his cigar as they walk. "Let's get that coffee, I've got something to sweeten it with." Tapping his jacket pocket.

CHAPTER 6

Later that evening, it is raining lightly now, as Jack drives his big black car slowly, along Frankford Avenue, under the elevated train tracks. His windshield wipers, slowly moving across the glass, as Jack peers into the shadowy darkness of the many boarded up store fronts, and trash filled recessed doorways. Revealing prostitutes in the shadows, coming out of hiding, to show their wares to the passing cars.

While other more desperate prostitutes, are looking hopefully at the passing cars, exposing themselves, and yelling to the occupants to stop, and then returning to hide within the shadows, at the approach of suspected police cars.

Jack is looking at the young sexy prostitutes, drinking a can of beer as he drives. A paper bag, containing the remains of a six pack of beer, sits on the floor besides the seat. Pulling up at a seedy looking corner, his car now intermittently illuminated by a flashing neon sign, Jack exits, and walks across the street, through the rain, towards the bar. Pulling up the collar, of his old chocolate colored leather jacket, as he walks under the, "Blue Magic – Go Go Bar" sign, and enters through the front door. He finds an empty seat at the bar, removes his jacket, hangs it on the back of the bar stool, and placing a twenty-dollar bill on the bar in front of him, sits down. As the scantily clad barmaid approaches him, he orders a Heineken bottle of beer, and an Irish whiskey.

Later a slightly drunk Jack, is sitting at the bar staring at his drink, while his change from a twenty-dollar bill, is on the bar, piled up in front of him. A beautiful scantily clad, dancer is on the platform, moving to the music's beat, and she is watching Jack, and his money. While another gorgeous dancer, is moving through the crowd, seeking tips by dancing for the individual men, one at a time.

Later that night, a visually drunk Jack picks up his remaining money from the bar, grabs his leather jacket from the back of his chair, tips the barmaid a few dollar bills, and walks slowly toward the door. As he exits the bar, "Blue Magic" flashes above, and on to Jack's head, from the neon sign above, as he tries to negotiate the rain, and the steps. He staggers across the street, beneath the cover of the elevated train tracks, as the sound of an approaching elevated train is rumbling toward him, from above. In the dimly lighted street Jack opens his big black car's door, crawls onto the front seat, and immediately falls asleep.

Still later, rain is pounding on to the sidewalks as a big black car drives slowly north. The car protected from the storm, because of the elevated train tracks above. The car is driving through the darkness as it approaches the corner, and then drives slowly on.

The rain has slowed down to a trickle now, and the prostitutes are visible again, as they are walking along the avenues shadowed corners, waving down the cars. The big black car, stops beside a gorgeous young long dark haired girl, dressed to kill, as the window goes down.

The young prostitute yells out to the car, "Hey baby, wanna have a date?" As she approaches the car awkwardly negotiating her way through the trash littered street, in her high heeled shoes.

The big black car's window goes back up and as the car drives away, and quickly disappears into the darkness of the night, there is no sign of the young prostitute.

The rain has subsided now, and as the cloud filled night sky seems to clear, the moon appears from between the departing clouds. Casting its pale light, on to the winding road, as it snakes its way along the tree lined East River Drive, its eerie light twinkling, and flashing on to the shimmering surface of the Schuylkill River.

As a big black car, comes into view, speeding along the East River Drive, beside the fast moving Schuylkill River. Driving through the rain swollen streets, shrouded by the wind battered trees. Heading toward the wooded section of the city, where the skeletal remains of the little children, and their mothers battered bodies are being found.

CHAPTER 7

Sunday morning finds Jack sitting on the steps of the old boarded up building, up the street from Pete's Place, watching cars go by at the corner. Drinking a bottle of beer, and at his feet a raggedy looking old dog, that has befriended him. As Jack quietly pets his new found friend, he despondently looks at his hands, holding his beer. He is in deep thoughts, with a disheveled look about him.

The dog lays at Jack's feet, contentedly looking up at him. Jack gives him some of his beer in his cupped hand, smiling at the dog as it laps it up.

"There you go killer."

As Jack returns his attention to the passing cars at the corner, and the dog falls asleep at his feet, his thoughts return to the past. He cannot forget the past, and move on with his life, because there is no resolution to his situation. Jack is an extremely loyal person who sees good in just about everyone, which is surprising because his work takes him into some of the worst situations, that humans can possibly do to the innocent people of this world.

It is not that Jack is naive, but it is just that his kindness, his outlook towards the people of this world is based on his unshakable belief that people are inherently good. That in their heart, is a goodness that we are all born with. That they would do good towards other people, if they could, but being poor, and maybe never having had a chance to succeed, in this cruel world, they become cruel like this world. Jack's thoughts always seem to revert to this line of thinking.

The what-ifs, what if his family had not been taken from him, what if he had not gone to work that morning, what if their disappearance had never happened. It is the what-ifs that are slowly killing Jack.

Later the quiet of the night is broken by the sound of a motor revving, as Jack starts his car. He begins to drive off, but then he thinks he sees something in his rear view mirror, an unusual black shadowy figure, that seemed to move when he started to drive off....

... And when he looks again, it is gone.

Jack pulls up in front of the Fishtown Diner, and stopping his car, gets out and starts to go inside. Furtively looking about as he walks, again he thinks he sees a black shadowy figure that appears to move, off in the darkness of the night.

Jack appears not to notice, as he opens the door, and starts to walk in. Then stopping suddenly, he quickly turns, and peers into the black shadows, then after a time, seeing nothing he enters the dinner.

Jack stops at the cash register and grabs some packets of jelly from a basket beside it. He then goes to the middle of the counter and sits down on a stool, picking up the menu as he does so.

One of the double doors leading from the kitchen opens, and a young, pretty waitress comes out carrying a tray of clean coffee cups. She puts the tray down, on a similar stack of clean cups, and notices Jack sitting there and smiles.

Jack, who is still pretending to be looking at the menu, looks up as she approaches. Smiling at the young

40

girl Jack closes the menu. The waitress walks up, bringing a cup of coffee, puts the cup down in front of Jack, smiles at him and taking out her check book as she speaks, begins to write out Jack's order, as she has a hundred times before.

"Well, have you made up your mind Jack?"

"What's the special Angela?"

"Come on Jack," smiling playfully, "don't kid me, what do you want?"

"What?" Pretending to be shocked, "you think I'm trying to be funny here! Come on, you know me better than that"

"Jack!"

Jack is smiling at her playfully, drinking his coffee. "What's the big deal, oh by the way I don't need jelly with my coffee." Handing her a packet of jelly that's lying on Jack's saucer, that was not there a moment ago when she brought it to him.

"Jack! Don't try to pull that old trick on me again, okay." Handing her back the stolen stuff. "What me?..." gently taking her delicate little hand in his hands. "You know I wouldn't play with you, now how bout my food, okay? Please."

"Okay Jack," rolling her eyes, and looking right at him, "Now, what do you want to eat?"

"Oh, you know ... what I always order, the meat loaf."

A smiling Angela, shows Jack what she wrote down on his check when he first came in. The check book reads ...

... "Meatloaf, mas pot, str bn's, grav r&b, beer." She leans in putting her head on her hands, elbows on the counter, and is smiling at Jack. She then lightly pats him on his cheek as she says....

"See I know you Jack Ramsey." Saying this she muses up his hair, laughing as she walks off.

41

"I'll get your beer Jack," and disappears into the kitchen. Sipping his coffee Jack smiles at her as she walks away, but a sadness soon overwhelms Jack as he watches her go through the swinging doors ...

... and a now despondent Jack watches his coffee cup, and thinks of other things.

Later that night as the moonlight filters eerily into Jack's cramped disheveled room, a restlessly sleeping Jack is dreaming. Seemingly fending off something, murmuring as he sleeps.

CHAPTER 8

Pale opaque purple mountains, off in the distance, are almost shrouded from view, by the menacingly dark clouds, which seem to loom over this sleepy little tree filled town, as the darkness fills the air with a foreboding of evil.

And on one of these tree lined streets, a look into one of the windows on this melancholy block of homes reveals....

A sadly deep in thought, lovely young woman. Sheila sits folding children clothes. The TV is on, but the sound is but a murmur. Her three little girls sit on the floor quietly playing a board game, as they alternately, try to smile at their mother.

Later Sheila is in the process of tucking her four-year-old daughter Nicole into bed, as she kisses her youngest child good night. Then puts out the lights, but when she is at the door leaving the room, she hears.

"Please leave the light on mommy." Sheila kisses her daughter again, and turns on a small night light.

"Good night honey bun," and starts to leave.

Nicole is now smiling happily at her mother, and pulls the covers around herself. Sheila smiles, a sad smile, as she closes the door half way behind her, and then walks to her bedroom, closing the door behind her, as the muffled sound of someone crying behind the door is heard.

As morning comes, Sheila is getting dressed, she despondently looks about the room, picking up an old silver framed picture, of a smiling older woman, standing behind Sheila's three little children, who are seated on a photographer's bench. As Sheila holds the picture, she tries not to cry, but tears well up in her eyes, and she breaks down crying uncontrollably. Sheila's eldest little child, Carol appears at the doorway and timidly approaches her mother, very slowly, as her other daughter, Heather looks on quietly from the doorway. Upon reaching her mother, Carol puts her arms around her mother, gently holding her. Sheila turns to her, and kneeling down clings to her, continuing to cry.

"Don't cry mommy, grand mom is in heaven now, she won't be in any more pain, now mommy." As she gently strokes her mother's honey colored hair.

"I know honey. I know ..."

CHAPTER 9

On another tree lined street, in this little town, sits
another old front porch home. Where a white back
dropped, discreetly lit sign, "Mulligan 's Funeral Home,"
marks the entrance to the driveway. Which is filled with
cars parked off to the one side, as it winds its way up to
the home's porch front, and then back down to the street
again.

Jack parks his car out on the street, and then
walks up the main steps, and on to the front porch,
carrying an enveloped Mass Card in his hand. Suit
jacketed older men, walk about smoking, talking quietly
outside on the large porch. Jack smiles at them
accommodatingly, in an attempt to be friendly, to the
men. Not recognizing anyone, he hesitatingly enters the
opened, old ornately scrolled, wooden doubled doors.

Jack signs the opened book, resting on a small
raised podium, takes a religious card of his wife's sisters
death notification, a small prayer card, and leaves his
Mass Card on top of a small pile of envelopes, on a table
beside the podium. Jack passes by the rising wooden
spindled staircase, down the chair lined hallway, toward
the partially people filled room.

Jack walks by rows of empty, steel folding
chairs, past the seated mourners, and pauses as he
watches Sheila and her little girls, sitting quietly looking
toward the opened casket, a sleeping child in Sheila's
arms. Then Jack approaches the lovely flowered
baskets, and flowered sprays adorning the opened
casket. Looking down at the older women before him, he

49

rests his hand on her cold hands holding her rosaries. Jack stands there a long time, then kneels down, and says a silent prayer. Holds her hands again, and leans over and kisses her on the forehead.

He then turns and walks over to a quietly crying Sheila who is holding her sleeping little child Nicole, as Nicole awakens, and looks up at Jack.

Jack hugs Sheila tenderly, and staring at Nicole, thinks to himself. "My god, she looks exactly like my little Nicole did when she disappeared … "

"I'm your Uncle Jack." Jack kneels down and holds Sheila and her little girl tenderly.

Later people are almost all gone now, and Jack is holding a sleeping Nicole, standing outside by the funeral homes porch railing, getting some fresh air, watching people go.

Jack looks back into the funeral home, and sees Sheila kneeling beside her mother's coffin. Jack shakes his head, and starts to cry again quietly, turning away from the few people there.

Jack looks down at Nicole, who he is still tenderly holding in his arms, he is trying not to cry, as he carefully moves her hair away from her eyes.

He holds her to himself, gently rocking her, shaking his head slowly, mumbling, as he cries softly to himself.

Later outside the funeral home, standing beside Sheila's car, as he is helping her to get her kids into her old car, he kisses her cheek, and holds her tenderly.

"Thanks for coming Uncle John,"

"I'm sorry it had to be like this."
"Want to come over to the house."
"Sure, but just call me Jack. Okay."
"Okay Jack."
"Okay, but your still my little girl."
"I'm glad you're here, Uncle Jack."
"Just Jack"
"Okay, Jack."

CHAPTER 10

Sheila, and her children are quietly sitting around the kitchen table eating Kentucky Fried Chicken, Jack is drinking a beer.

"Thanks for the chicken, Uncle Jack."

Sheila looks at her children, and motions for them to thank their Uncle Jack.

"Thank you Uncle Jack," Carol and Heather stumble out together, but Nicole can't remember Jack's name.

"Thank you Uncle ..."

The other girls laughingly say.

"Uncle Jack ... "

Nicole has turned her head, and is angrily looking at them as she says.

"Thank you ... Uncle Jack."

Smiling kindly at her.

"You are all very welcome."

"Can you stay over tonight?" Sheila asks Jack.

Nicole hugs him as she asks, "Please Uncle Jack."

Jack takes out a tooth brush from his jacket pocket, and smiles as he shows it to the girls.

"I was hoping you'd ask ... yes, thank you."

"Good, would you like another beer?"

"I'll get it mommy," Nicole hops off the chair and runs toward the refrigerator.

"Walk, don't run honey, you'll get hurt."

That night, Carol and Heather are kissing their mother, and Jack good night, as they leave to go to bed. Following them out into the hallway, Jack is trailing behind, while carrying a sleeping Nicole. Jack kisses Nicole on the forehead, as he is putting her into bed, and covering her up. He then stands there a long time watching her, Sheila's child Carol comes up beside Jack, and tugs at his sleeve. Jack looks down at her, picks her up, kisses her on the cheek, and they leave the bedroom together.

Later under a moonless night sky, standing outside in Sheila's backyard, Jack looks around and while holding Sheila gently, his head drops against her head.

"It's nice out here." They stand talking quietly while looking about in the yard. Then after a few minutes they go back into the house, through the rear doorway into the kitchen. Looking through Sheila's kitchen window we see them, talking animatedly. Jack is sitting at the kitchen table.

Sheila brings him another cold bottle of Heineken, "Here's your beer Uncle Jack."

"Thanks," taking the beer, "you don't know, but … ah, I was an orphan," as he pauses he looks into Sheila's beautiful blue eyes, and then looks away.

"I never had a family growing up in the orphanage, but I'd like to be a part of one, if it's okay?" Sheila smiles at Jack.

"You already are Uncle Jack ..." A long pause ensues, quietly looking down, as she talks.

"I don't know if I believe in anything anymore, why things happen the way they do, I mean the good people suffer, and the bad, well … " tears roll down her face as she tries not to cry.

"It's not fair."

"I know Sheila, I know. Life is ... I don't know," awkwardly looking down and unconsciously turning the gold wedding ring on his finger, as he talks.

"You know when your mother was a young woman like yourself. Her sister, my wife Diane, was only a young girl, and your mother took her out, and ... well I don't know if you know how poor they were. Your grandfather was sick with black lung disease, and had been for years, because he worked in the coal mines for all those years, up in Scranton." Shaking her head, in acknowledgement.

"I know, I have a picture of my mother on a pony, and there is a very steep street in the back ground, and a church steeple, but I don't know where it was."

Jack looking down at his ground.

"Yeah, I saw that one, she was so cute."

"She was a beautiful little girl, reminds me of my Heather,"

"Yeah she was beautiful," Smiling at Sheila in a strangely quiet way.

"What?"

"She looked like you, when you were little," smiling sadly, "well anyway, your mother bought her younger sister, my wife Diane, a complete outfit. Shoes, stockings, frilly dress, jacket, handbag, and Diane wanted to carry all the packages herself. She was a sweet young girl, and you know they didn't have much money, when they were growing up," looking at Sheila now.

"Well, anyway, your aunt was so happy about what your mother had done for her that she got all excited and," looking down as he speaks. "She put the packages down, and left them alone for a moment to follow your mother, and when she returned all the packages were gone, someone had stolen all her new clothes."

Continuing to turn his wedding ring around, and around on his finger, with the fingers of his other hand as he speaks, while hiding his gaze from Sheila.

"She cried, and cried, and tried to apologize to your mother, because she had lost all the presents," wiping away tears from his eyes as he speaks ...

... "Well, you know what your mother did, she went back to all those stores and bought them all again, every last thing, and she kissed her, and told her to be happy, and to never cry over spilt milk. She said life was too short." Looking at Sheila now, who is also crying quietly....

"Sheila, I don't know why I thought of that, but well I always loved your mother too you know."

"That's a nice story about my mom, thanks, Uncle Jack"

"Just Jack, okay."

"Okay."

A quiet silence ensues, both of them sitting there, Jack drinking slowly, watching each other with a happy sad kind of smile. As Jack is finishing his beer, Sheila says.

"Maybe we should get some sleep." Both get up, and hug each other emotionally, Jack almost whispers, "I guess you're right."

"I made up a bed for you on the couch, Okay?"

"Thanks, it's fine, I'll be fine."

They walk toward the living room. Jack puts his arm around her shoulder, as they walk. She Kisses Jack's cheek.

"Good night Uncle Jack."

"Good night baby."

That night, a sleeping Jack is fighting off something, while he is sleeping on the living room sofa, he is mumbling something, under his breath, and there is fear in his voice.

At the same moment, a sleeping Nicole suddenly sits up in bed, although still asleep and fending off something, suddenly screaming, "Help me, mommy, mommy ..."

A awakened Sheila jumps out of bed, and fearfully thinking the worst, runs down the hallway, and into Nicole's bedroom, while a violently terrified Nicole is screaming for her.

"Please help me mommy," Sheila hurries to her daughters bed, and tries to comfort her. Holding her daughter, as her other two daughters come into Nicole's bedroom.

Jack is following them into the room, not knowing what to do, looking fearful of what is wrong he asks, "Is she all right?"

Sheila doesn't hear him as she tenderly holds her screaming daughter, trying to comfort her frightened child, "It's all right honeybun, it's all right, it was a bad dream. I'm here now, don't cry honeybun, don't cry ..."

Later as Sheila holds and slowly rocks, back and forth, a now calmly sleeping Nicole, Sheila is staring at nothing, and crying quietly.

Still later that night Jack cannot sleep, too many disturbing thoughts keep rushing into his restlessly troubled mind, unable to go back to sleep. So he is sitting at the kitchen table drinking a beer, quietly thinking to himself, and looking out the window. As the wind blows the trees about in the yard, and the rain torrentially beats against the window pane.

Early the next morning, we hear the birds chattering to each other, as dawn is breaking through the reddening sky filled clouds, above the pale almost opaque purple looking mountains off in the distance.

Jack is trying to shave, but while staring at himself in the steamy bathroom's mirror, his eyes are welling up with tears, and he silently starts to cry, steadying himself against the sink, as he tries to control himself.

Eventually morning comes, and with it a kind of tranquility. Sheila has just finished cooking breakfast, and it is unusually quiet, as Jack and Sheila's girls are eating a breakfast of hot cakes and sausage. A tired looking Sheila sits down with them, bringing her coffee, and starts to eat her breakfast.

CHAPTER 11

It is raining lightly as the funeral cars are lining up outside Saint Laurentius Church. Mourners follow the casket from the hearse, up the steps, and into the church. Some people were already there waiting for the Mass. Jack holds Nicole's little hand, as he follows behind Sheila, who is holding her children to her, walking behind the casket, moving down the aisle toward the church's alter.

The Funeral Mass is progressing along as the priest is now blessing the casket, with the smoking incense, and softly saying a prayer in Latin. Sheila holds tighter on to Carol's hand, as she tries not to cry, but tears are welling up in her eyes, as the sound of the church soloist, singing up in the balcony, fills the church. While Nicole is standing up, on the pew, looking back sheepishly, and peeking over the back of the pew up at the balcony.

The Funeral Mass is over now, and the mourners are following a quietly crying Sheila, and her children, as she follows her mother's casket to the rear of the church, and down the church steps. The pall bearers carrying the casket, to the waiting hearse, slide it into the back of the hearse, as the rain is increasing. The umbrellas are opening as the mourners are exiting the church. It is now raining heavily as the hearse, and limousine pull away from the church, while funeral flagged cars follow behind, in the steadily increasing storm.

Following a soggy drive through the city, the rain is still pounding onto the windshield, as the hearse pulls through the opened wrought iron gate, beneath the black cast iron, Holy Cross Cemetery sign. Then snaking its way through the cemetery's narrow lanes, beside the tombstone filled landscape, stopping eventually at a freshly dug grave.

After the casket is carried to its resting place, and the mourners gather around the grave site, beneath a lightly falling rain. The priest prays over the casket, and afterword's a crying Sheila walks up to the casket holding a single rose, and then lays it on top, touching the casket tenderly with her fingers, as she cries ...

"Bye mom, I love you, God bless you ... " now speaking in an almost inaudible volume, "I'll miss you mom, bye bye." She runs her fingers along the casket, as she is walking away until her fingers can no longer touch her mother's casket.

Sheila's children also approach, following their mother, with their roses. Then one at a time they lay them on top, crying as they bid their grand mom goodbye. While Jack is holding Nicole's little hand waiting in the slender line, to say goodbye. Fingering his rose's stem absentmindedly as he and Nicole lay their roses on top, and Jack tenderly touches the casket.

Driving away from the grave site, a deeply disturbed Sheila is crying, holding her head, while Carol is holding on to her mother, and Heather is also crying sitting next to Jack.

Nicole has squirmed her way to be standing up on the rear seat, and looking out through the rear window, back at the grave site. While holding onto the top of the back of the seat, as she stares transfixed on the grave, she sees a small trail of Gray Blue Smoke rising from the grave site, slowly in a column going straight up, into the air above.

Watching intently, she is frightened, but cannot turn away. She continues to watch the Gray Blue Smoke rising into the sky. She keeps looking back as the limousine drives away, and out of the cemetery, under the black Holy Cross Cemetery signs gated exit.

CHAPTER 12

Later back at Sheila's house, people are mingling with each other, talking, drinking, eating, looking out of the windows, trying to forget, but they cannot. They're laughing at unfunny jokes, and feeling uncomfortable, while trying to act comfortable.

As a kindly looking woman approaches Sheila quietly, respectfully. "I hope I'm not intruding on you," hugging her, "if you need me don't hesitate to call, okay?"

Sheila nods her head, speaking quietly. "Thanks Audrey, thanks for coming."

Jack is standing by himself, looking out into Sheila's yard, despondently thinking of the past. When Nicole comes timidly up to him, watching him quietly, and holds his hand. Jack turns unexpectedly and seeing her standing there he softens, smiling as he stoops, and holds her tenderly. She asks hesitatingly …

"Will you come to my birthday party Uncle Jack?"

"Thank you Nicole, I'd love to come to your birthday party, let's go ask your mommy." Jack kisses her as he picks her up, and holds her to him.

Jack carries Nicole as he walks over to where Sheila is standing. "I'd like to come to Nicole's birthday party, if it's okay?"

"Sure," smiling, "how about another beer?"

"I'll get it mommy." Jack puts a squirming Nicole down, and she laughingly runs into the kitchen for him.

"Walk."

Later that night, at Sheila's front door, Sheila is hugging Jack, and kisses his cheek, as she is bidding him goodbye. He kisses the girls, then he gets into his car, and lowers the window as he closes the door.

"Good bye Sheila, girls, thank you. Hope to see you soon, bye ... bye."

"God bless, watch your driving Uncle Jack. Thanks for coming ..."

Jack waves goodbye, as he drives away, while Sheila gathers her children to her, and still waving watches him drive off. Nicole also is waving goodbye.

"Bye, bye Uncle ... Jack."

CHAPTER 13

A car is sitting in the darkness, buried in the woods off on an old dirt road, beneath a full moon lit sky. It is too dark to see their faces, but a young woman, and her little daughter are trying to start their car. As the key turns, the sound of quick clicking is heard, but their car's engine doesn't even try to start. Exiting their car, and standing outside in the dark with their hood up, and looking at the road up at the corner. After fruitless attempts to start her car, the young woman, closes the hood of the car, and she starts to walk away with her daughter.

A car's headlights, making a U-turn at the corner, illuminates them temporarily, freezing hope on their faces, which then fades quickly as it drives away. It is the waitress Angela, from the Fishtown Diner Jack likes, with her little daughter. Angela and her little daughter, decide to leave the car.

"I guess we'll have to walk home honey, come on it will be fun." Walking away from the car at this point, continuing along the path, into the darkness of the woods, above the Boat House Row area by the Schuylkill River.

But something is watching Angela and her daughter as they walk deeper into the woods, following a lonely looking path. Seeing them in black and white, and like in tunnel vision. Following them from within the dense woods, and looking at them through the brush. While the sound of a heart beating, pounding, and heavy breathing, or panting like a large dog, or a wolf, is heard as it is following them.

As they enter a particularly densely wooded area behind the Art Museum, and above the river on a small lonely looking path, her weary little child says to her mother.

"I'm tired mommy"

"I know honey, you're tired, we'll take this short cut home."

"But I'm very tired mommy." Picking up her daughter.

"I know baby, but let's hurry faster and we'll get home quicker."

But something is quickly coming up from behind them, watching them hurrying along the narrow path, while the growing sound of a heart beating, pounding is heard, and quickly gaining ground on them, growling loudly. Angela turns hearing the sound of something growling behind her, and looks back down the path they have just walked. Staring into the darkness behind her, she sees nothing at first, but a few seconds later she sees it.

A shadowy, mythical looking demon like apparition, in a purple black peaked monk like robe, quickly approaching her. The folds of the long robe blowing open into the air like a black cape, trailing behind it, as its burning yellow eyes gleam from within the darkness of the robes peaked hood.

Watching them, seeing them in a kind of black and white tunnel vision, as it is running up behind them. Its heart beating, pounding faster and faster, and loud growling is now heard. It is so dark her face is barely visible, as she sees it. Horrified she is backing up, still holding her child's hand, trying to scream but she cannot move, she is screaming but, no sound is coming out.

70

Quickly gaining ground on her as she starts to turn, and run away, but it is on her as she is turning. The horrific looking demon's old wrinkled, sharp finger nailed hands, grappling her to the ground. Another sound, one of deep diabolical laughter, also interrupts the night, and continues softly, as the child watches her ravaged mother's body being pulled into total darkness, leaving a blood soaked bloody trail.

The child sits on the ground, in an apparent state of shock, blank eyes staring out ahead of her, as a dark shadow falls over the little girl, and then it engulfs her, lifts her up, and carries her into the woods beside the path. Another sound, one of deep groaning, and laughter continues softly, as crunching is also heard, coming from the darkness of the woods.

CHAPTER 14

Sheila is standing just inside the bedroom door watching her little girl sleeping fretfully. Nicole's dreaming, and it is scary to watch her, because she is seemingly fending off something in her dream. Sheila sits down by her little girl watching her sleep, and although tired she watches over her little child, as Sheila's other two children come into Nicole's bedroom groggily, rubbing their eyes. They stand, quietly, watching Nicole struggling with her dreams tormentors.

After a sleepless night, Sheila is cooking her children breakfast, and then after taking a needed break, goes to their bedrooms to awaken them. After a few minutes her children start to straggle, one by one, into the kitchen, and take their places at the table. While they quietly await their breakfast they are obviously tired, from the lack of sleep, having been awakened all night.

      A tired looking Sheila is now done cooking, and is serving her children breakfast. They are all eating their breakfast quietly, without any talking between them.

        *   *   *

The police station is just as busy as the other day, as numerous detectives are talking to each other, sitting at their desks, walking about, typing, talking on the phones, drinking coffee, and creating quite a commotion, but Jack does not seem to hear anything, he is seated at his desk, staring in front of him intently examining the numerous documents.

There are pictures of the remains of the latest murdered child, from different angles, but they are partially covered up by the reports of the Doc. Also pictures of the grave site and the surrounding area, and the woods behind her and in front. The files are laid out on top of the other stacks of files, of the other murdered children's folders. He has shifted some of them, into the boxes on the floor, beside his desk. He is clean shaven this time, but looks very tired, as he is examining this and other documents spread out before him.

Doc's autopsy report on the remains of the latest little girl, reveals she was about three, or four years old, and that she had laid in that grave about three weeks. As Jack reads the Doc's notes, sipping a container of coffee, and looking over everything, his restless tired eyes reveal that he has no answers.

Thinking out loud, Jack mumbles as he reads. "There was no blood in the soil beneath the child's body, and there were no fragments of clothing found either," making notations as he reads. "Meaning she was dead some time before she was buried there, and she was naked when she was. Her rib cage was crushed, and some of her organs and bones are missing."

Jack's so involved in his own thoughts, that he doesn't even hear the other detective when he comes up behind him, and puts his hand on Jack's shoulder.

"Jack."

Jack looks up, to see Detective Richard Thompson standing there.

"They've found another child's body Jack, here is the location, she was found by the cadaver dogs, back in the same woods.

"Thanks Dick."

Detective Thompson leaves a slip of paper on Jack's desk and walks off. Jack stands up, and as he does, puts some order to his case, puts them back into their folders, then puts them into the top drawer of his desk, and locks it. He then picks up his note book, takes the slip of paper, grabs his jacket off of the back of the chair and moves toward the door, forgetting his coffee.

Captain Shaw watches Jack leave, with a grimace of disgust, opens a note book, and glancing at the time, writes down something at the bottom of the notation filled page. He then looks about the room.

"Detective Johnson, come in here."

Detective Johnson follows Shaw into his office, Shaw then closes the door, and indicates for Detective Johnson to sit down, he does. Shaw walks behind the desk, removes his jacket, and without sitting down confronts Johnson.

"I want you to start to tail that son of a bitch, starting tonight."

"Who?"

"Ramsey, that son of a bitch, Jack Ramsey. Now go home, get some sleep, and tail him every night from here on out until I tell you to stop ... You Got That."

A cruel smile breaks out on Detective Johnson's face. "I'll nail that son of a bitch."

"Good," showing Detective Johnson to the door, "I want daily reports, so I can arrest him, as soon as we get anything." Putting his hand on Johnson's shoulder, "Now go out and Nail That Murdering Bastard."

*　　　　　*　　　　　*

At her front door Sheila is kissing her children goodbye, as they start off for school, walking together quietly, while Sheila is watching them walk off out of sight.

Carol and Heather are gradually continuing to walk further and further ahead of Nicole. Because they are walking normally, and she is walking slowly, and in deep thought. They turn and wait for her, waiting patiently, as Nicole awakens from her deep thoughts, and runs to catch up. They cross the street, walking together now alongside an aged, black spiked, wrought iron estate fencing, bordering Palmer Cemetery, an old revolutionary war cemetery, in neglected disrepair.

Sheila walks across the street toward her neighbor's kitchen door. Knocking at the door, and then going in.
          "Audrey ... it's me Sheila, are you home?"
          "Yeah, one-second Sheila." A despondent Sheila sits down. Wringing her hands as she waits. Approaching sounds of footsteps, hurriedly coming down the stairs, awakens Sheila's attention.
          "Hi stranger," hugging her, "I'm so sorry honey."
          "Thanks," Sheila looks about nervously, "I overheard you say that you're looking for work. I'm going to have to go to back, to work any day now, and I was wondering if, well if you wouldn't mind baby-sitting my little girls for me, I could pay what ..."
          "I would be very happy to watch over your little girls."
          "Thank you Audrey."
          Pouring a cup of coffee as she talks. "Have a cup of coffee? I've some homemade cake left."

76

Later that day, Nicole crosses the street, to Palmer Cemetery, heading home from her school. At an opening between the black iron bars of the fence, she ducks through the hole, like she normally does, every afternoon, on her way home from school. As she walks, she picks some of the wild flowers that are growing between, and among the aging tombstones, whose exacting lines run perpendicular in all directions.

CHAPTER 15

Jack is walking through a multi colored tree filled forest. Down a steep hill, at the bottom of which, is yellow crime scene tape, stretching around a vast area, including the hill on which Jack walks. Uniformed policemen, and white paper outfitted policemen are at work, searching out the perimeter of the crime scene.

"Lieutenant," a policemen points, "we found another body, maybe it's the child's mother." He and Jack walk carefully to where the body lies, partially covered by leaves heaped up into a kind of hill, between the rough brush at the bottom of the hill.

"Thanks." Jack looks down at the bloody partially nude body of a woman, who is starting to decompose.

"Lieutenant." Jack turns to see the same policeman, pointing in the direction of the child's body.

"The child's over here." The policeman then walks off to join the others at the perimeter of the area they are searching.

Still looking down at the woman's body, Jack shakes his head sadly. Thinking out loud …

… "She'd been torn to pieces, literally torn to pieces, battered black and blue. Her bones were broken, so many broken bones, like she was hit by a truck. The ground was drenched with her blood."

He then walks carefully though the brush to where the little child's body lies. Jack kneels down, crosses himself, and says a silent prayer, mumbling as he does so. He stands up uneasily, and remains looking at the child's body, thinking out loud.

"She'd also been brutally murdered, her torn and broken body had been mauled by something. A dog, I guessed at the time. Her little white dress soaked in so much blood, I didn't think it could have had been just hers. Her rib cage was ripped apart, her vital organs were exposed, and it seemed some were missing from her body, but there was so much bloody goo, it was impossible for me to know if they were there, Doc would know, he'll know ..."

Jack's head is bowed, shivering slightly as he looks down at the child's body. A policeman approaches Jack, and seems to be talking to him, but Jack shows no sign of a reply. The policeman gives up and walks off, leaving Jack alone staring down into the shallow earthen grave.

Doc walks up to Jack and gently puts his hand on his shoulder, Jack turns and sees it is him. Jack looks at him momentarily.

"Hi Doc," and then returns his gaze to the child. Doc relights his cigar and looks at Jack.

"You want a cigar, Jack?"

"No thanks Doc, what I need is a drink, and some sleep."

Doc walks to the foot of the child's shallow grave, "I didn't have to be a mind reader to know that, Jack."

Jack drops his head into his hands, while looking into the child's shallow grave...

"You know, when I was young, I was afraid of the dark, and look at me now," puffing on his cigar, "I live with the dead every day ..."

"Time Jack, just time, that's all."

The crimson colored sky is beginning to darken, following the sun's decent behind the quickly darkening tree line, above the area where the child's body was found this morning. While Jack and the white paper suited police, are still looking for clues, among the over grown bushes and paths in the area.

While the flashing lights of the police cars are crowded together up on the hill, Jack's car sits alone in a darkened area waiting for its master to return.

Unobtrusively under a tree, off in the distance, Detective Johnson sits, watching Jack's car intently, in his unmarked patrol car, smoking quietly, while listening to country music being played on a small portable radio. Detective Johnson reaches into the glove compartment, and extracts a pint of whiskey and takes a long drink, before he stops. A look on the floor of his car reveals a pile of empty crumpled beer cans, and an empty box of donuts.

CHAPTER 16

Under the playgrounds numerous bank of lights, Nicole and her sisters are playing on a merry go round. Going around and around in circles they fly, their innocent joy is intoxicating, as they laughingly play. Sheila watches them as they play, smiling sadly. While someone, or something else is also watching, but as if in like a black and white tunnel vision ...

... Watching them playing ...

*   *   *

Later in Pete's Place, Jack sits alone looking into his drink, which he holds with both hands on the bar, deep in thought. Also on the bar, there is his note book, which is closed. He finishes his whiskey, picks up his note book, taps it against his fist, and stares into the mirror behind the bar.

Charlie, the night bartender, approaches.
"Another one Jack?"
Jack nods his head, and continues to look at himself in the mirror, as Charlie brings Jack a cold bottle of Heineken, and a bottle of Irish whiskey. Pouring out Jacks whiskey, he takes some bills from the bar, puts the bottle back in its place on the rack, and walks to the other end of the bar, where he returns to his newspaper.

Jack is holding his head, talking to himself, under his breath, barely audible, and still staring into the mirror at the strange looking man who is staring back.

"Poor child," he mumbles to himself, almost unintelligibly, "Poor child, poor murdered, child, poor kids, five, five murdered children, five murdered children, past year, all butchered, and found in the park, same park. I don't know, I just don't know ..." As he drinks his whiskey, he quietly asks himself the same question, over and over to himself. "Why ... why ... why ... why?" As Jack looks at himself in the mirror, his mind starts to drift off to a better time, after a while, Jack's dreaming ...

... Of lying beside his daughter, reading her, her favorite book, "The Little Prince." Holding Nicole tenderly while he reads to her, and she holding her Janie, and looking at her father. Apparently finished now, he closes the book, and puts it down, on the bed beside him.

Nicole is watching a gold charm bracelet on her little wrist, and then turns and hugs her father and kisses him, jiggling the bracelet.

"I love you daddy. Thank you so much for my birthday present I love it daddy ... daddy, can you please read me that story again, daddy, please daddy." Jack kisses his daughter's neck and she starts to laugh.

"Okay pumpkin, all right, but you know it's past your bedtime." Jack's pretending to act very sternly. "All right, but never, ever again, do you understand." Nicole hugs her father, and laughs hysterically.

"Oh thank you, thank you daddy. I love 'The Little Prince' so much, now start at the beginning okay?" Jack hugs and kisses his little daughter, holding her to himself. "I love you daddy, never let me go, okay."

"I'll never let you go away from me, my little pumpkin, never, never." Burying his face into her hair,

84

holding her gently. "I'll never let you go, never," whispering desperately, "never, never ..."

... In a blur, someone's hands are shaking Jack forcefully ... "Jack ... Jack ..."

... "Never," whispering, "never, never," Jack's dazed gaze is still staring into the mirror behind the bar.

"Jack ... Jack what the hell's gotten into you," Charlies shaking him by the shoulders, "are you all right?"

Jack gets up, stumbles, rights himself, holds on to the bar for stability and looks about the bar dazed and confused. Slowly as he realizes where he is, he grabs his six pack of beer, off the bar, and leaving money, he goes out into the street.

Talking to himself as he walks, stopping at the steps of the same old boarded up row house, up the street from Pete's bar. He sits down like before, staring down at the ground, drinking his beer.

An old man, who resembles Jack, watches him sitting there. The old man walks up to Jack, and puts his hand on his shoulder. Jack looks up at him, and there are tears in Jack's eyes, he's been crying. Jack buries his head into his hands, and quietly continues to cry. The old man sits down beside Jack.

"Come on home son, there's nothing here. Come on now, you can bring your beer." The old man helps Jack get up, and they walk off together towards Pete's Place, Jack is still clutching his beer.

In the darkness, up the street, Detective Johnson watches Jack stumbling back toward Pete's bar, guided by the old man. Detective Johnson writes something into his notebook, then takes a long drink of whiskey.

CHAPTER 17

In Jack's dark street light lit, shadowy room, a fully dressed Jack sits on his bed. Drinking a can of beer, staring at a spot on the floor beside his muddy shoes, and against the wall, sits Nicole's rag doll Janie, staring back, besides a small mountain of toys that fill that one corner of the room.

Jack drinks the last of his beer, and gets another from a paper bag on the floor. The sound of a pop is heard, as he opens the top of the can. He drinks a long time, finishes it, crumbles up the can, and puts it on the floor. He sits there, staring at the picture of his missing family, and then picks up his family's picture. He is staring at the picture, then placing the picture on the bed, he kneels on the floor while staring at it, and begins to pray.

"In the name of the Father," crossing himself as he speaks, "and of the Son, and of the Holy Ghost, Amen. Please dear Lord, please watch over my family, tonight dear Lord. Please dear God don't let anything happen to them. But if something has to happen, please let it go off to the side and miss them, and be only something small, please dear Lord watch out for them and keep them safe tonight dear God. And could you please watch out and protect my mother and father, and all my family and friends tonight dear Lord, and please, please help me to be a good person, dear God, you know in my heart I'd like to be a good person dear Lord, thank you dear God, Amen. In the name of the Father, and of the Son and of the Holy Ghost, Amen."

Jack starts to get up from his knees, hesitates and slips back to his knees.

"... And please dear God, return Diane and Nicole to me, or please, please take me dear Lord, let me die, thank you dear Lord." Crossing himself mumbling incoherently, as he is rising, he picks up the picture, sits on the bed again, and holding it to his heart he begins to softly cry.

*   *   *

Sheila's little Nicole is kneeling at her bedside, praying.

"God please look after my mother, and my sisters, and my grand mom Amen." She starts to get up and quickly kneels back down again.

"And please look after my Uncle Jack. Thank you dear Lord, good night.

" Nicole then happily jumps into bed. Sheila, who has been apparently standing there covers, her up, kisses her good night, and turns on the night light for her daughter.

"Good night honey bun. God bless."

"Thank you mommy good night."

Later, Nicole's murmuring under her breath, rolling around on her bed, seemingly fighting off something, and the bed seems to be lifting slightly, as Sheila comes into the room, and lies beside her troubled daughter.

*   *   *

While in Jack's dimly lit bedroom, above Pete's bar, he sleeps fitfully, mumbling under his breath as he sleeps.

CHAPTER 18

The next morning, Sheila's children are sitting at the kitchen table eating happily, smiling at their mother from time to time, as they finish their breakfast.

Later they quickly scurry about the house, gathering up their school books and supplies, and are getting dressed for school. Sheila is helping to pack her daughter's books into their school bags, and as they are now ready to leave for school, they are grouped together at the front door, kissing their mother goodbye.

Sheila waves good bye to her daughters, as they walk away down the street headed toward their school. Sheila smiles as she watches them walk off to school.

Heather and Carol are walking on the sidewalk, ahead of Nicole as they approach the corner. Across the street lies the tree lined centuries old, Palmer Cemetery. After waiting for Nicole to catch up, they cross the street, to the cemetery's corner.

The cemetery's main entrance, with its cobble stone drive way barred by its padlocked gate, lay off to the left along Palmer Street. Its stone gate house, and old oak tree filled landscape, offer foreboding disquiet for the children's imagination.

Beside the black wrought iron estate fencing surrounding the cemetery, along the tree lined street, tree roots are breaking through the faded crumbling red brick sidewalk.

As they walk, they come upon a wide gap between the iron bars. Carol and Heather look around, and then duck between the bars, at this break in the fence, and enter the cemetery's grounds. Nicole quickly follows them between the bars, and scampers toward her retreating sisters.

Walking across the wild looking, unkempt weed filled cemetery's lawn, beside the rows of tombstones, arching angels, Crosses, and mausoleums, they follow a familiar path worn into the grass. Winding between the tombstones and the trees, as they walk, they talk and laugh among themselves.

But a dark shadowed figure appears to be following them from afar, hidden from view among the shadows cast by the tombstones. Watching the little girls, as they walk. While off in the distance, past the children, on the horizon above the tree line, can be seen St. Laurentius Catholic Church's Cross topped spire.

As they reach the other side of the cemetery they follow the grassy path right to a hole in the fence, but before they can exit the cemetery, a large black alley cat crosses their path, it then stands back and watches them, hissing loudly at their approach. The girls cautiously exit the cemetery through the breach in the fence, suspiciously watching the large black alley cat as they do so.

They cross the street carefully, and then start to walk past the large Catholic Church. There a quiet young man is diligently working planting fresh flowers in the garden, from large cardboard boxes filled with young flowering plants.

Nicole is watching the young man, who is intently planting the piles of potted flowers, which are lying beside him. The young man looks up, and smiles to see the children walking by him. They smile back at him as they walk by, and then continue down the street. Nicole turns to wave to him, and he smiles as he waves back.

.

CHAPTER 19

Jack is talking to an older woman who is standing in the vestibule, Mrs. Stevens is visibly upset as she leads Jack into the house.

"I went to her house, this house, again this morning, only this time I brought a set of keys that she had given me, which I could not for the life of me find until this morning. There is no sign of my daughter, or granddaughter. It is like they just vanished."

Looking about the first floor of the house, as if to show the Lieutenant what she is saying, sitting down now, indicating for him to sit as well, Jack sits.

Mrs. Stevens is trying not to cry, "But the milk's sour, curdling, and the vegetables are starting to go bad." Suddenly standing and beginning to pace back and forth.

"That is not like my daughter to go away and not take care of those kinds of things before she had gone. She was supposed to go to Florida, for a week. But I could not remember the name of the motel she had given me, or the phone number so I could call her. And she did not call me, so I figured something came up, but when she did not call me after a few days I got worried, and came over here, but I could not get in," the older woman breaks down, and is openly crying now, "something is wrong, I know it, I just know it."

Jack is watching her intently, as he stands up, and glances out the open porch window. There is still a policeman outside, talking to a neighbor, beside his patrol car. Other neighbors across the street, are talking to each other in a little group, and watching the house.

Jack tenderly touches the crying woman's shoulder, and rubs her back gently, trying to comfort her. Jack speaks calmly and quietly, and asks. "Do you mind If I go upstairs, and look around Mrs. Stevens."

"No, no, you go do what you need to do Lieutenant," as she tries to compose herself.

Jack says, "Thank you," and walks up the steps, onto the stairway landings hallway, where he looks around, and then walks down the hallway, to what is apparently her daughter's bedroom. Jack enters the missing woman's bedroom, it is very clean and neat, except for a very slight covering of recent dust, that covers everything in the room. Jack runs his finger across the dresser top and leaves a very slight, but distinct mark upon it. The suitcases are open, half packed, and clothes apparently meant for the trip, left in small piles waiting to be packed in the cases on the bed.

Jack looks around the attractive room, opens a few drawers and looks inside. The clothes are neatly folded, orderly, and look to be in their place.

Jack looks into the remaining rooms, slowly but efficiently, he then starts to walk hesitantly down the stairs. Jack trudges down the last few steps, sits down next to Mrs. Stevens, who is trying to compose herself, and gently puts his arm around her.

"We'll see if we can find out what's going on. I promise you that, I promise I'll do everything I possibly can for you Mrs. Stevens." Jack stands up at this point, and starts for the front door.

Mrs. Stevens follows Jack to the door, "Thank you Lieutenant," looking around the room, as she speaks, "I cannot stay here any longer," giving Jack a framed picture of her daughter and her children. "Here they are together last Christmas." Handing him a picture she has removed from a group of pictures on the end table. She looks about the room again, and then she anxiously hands Jack the keys to the house.

Not taking his eyes off of Mrs. Stevens, Jack takes the items from her, and trying to comfort her, he tenderly places his hand on her shoulder as he does so.

"Her cars missing from the neighborhood also. I guess they told you that, do you need a description of her car?"

"No, we have it. Don't worry unnecessarily, go home, get some rest. I'll call when we get some news, try to get some sleep. Do you have someone to look after you?"

She shakes her head no, trying not to cry again, and without shaking his hand again. She turns and leaves the house, with Jack holding the daughter's keys, and the picture of her missing daughter, and child she had given him.

Jack watches her go out the door, down the steps, and following her on to the porch of the home. He watches her walk, head in her hands, wiping away tears, as she walks along the sidewalk down the street. Jack stays a little while longer, watching her disappear down the street, and he then reenters the home.

Jack begins methodically searching the whole house, from top to bottom. Looking into every possible corner to try to determine where, or what could have possibly have been her destination on the night of her disappearance. He decides to have someone check out her credit card purchases of the recent and preceding days of her disappearance, in the hope it will produce some sort of lead, that he can follow.

But Jack finishes his search unfruitfully, and with an almost hopeless despondency, he walks to the front door, giving the living room one last look around, before giving up, and locking the front door as he exits the house. He then walks over to the police officer across the street, to speak to him, before entering his black car, and driving away down the street.

Jack is driving through the Spring Garden section of the city, leaving the missing woman's house a few blocks behind, heading out toward the Art Museum, as he watches the passing neighborhoods, he is leaving behind, thinking to himself as he drives …

"Mrs. Stevens daughter is smaller than the body we'd found, days ago in Fairmount Park, and her child is older, taller than the child's body too. So we know that wasn't them, who we'd found, but it's in the same area."

Continuing to drive through the Art Museum area, turning onto the East River Drive … thinking to himself out loud ...

"The house with Mrs. Steven's missing daughter, and her child, are just a few miles south-east of the murder scene, we'd just found by the East River Drive, back deep in the woods, off the main road."

Watching the boats training for some upcoming race out on the Schuylkill River.

"I was sick in my stomach. I couldn't tell her how I knew, how she felt." Fumbling for a beer can from a paper bag on the floor of the car.

"I needed a bunch of drinks badly, and some sleep, but I wanted to see the latest crime scene again, things don't seem clean anymore."

The sound of the beer can's top pops, as he looks about with a forlorn hopelessness.

"I see dirt now where before I saw joy." Jack mumbles to himself.

As he drives along the East River Drive, he looks longingly at the tranquility of the river, and of the crew teams practicing on it.

98

CHAPTER 20

As the moon's eerily pale light, breaks through the cloud filled night sky, it creates forebodingly dark shadows thrust upon Philadelphia's monolithic city hall. Making it resemble some sort of medieval castle, with its towers climbing skyward. Its dark shadowed stone gargoyles, arches, massive stain glass windows and copper clad spires, surrounding the main stone tower soaring high above the rest. And atop its roof, rising even higher upon the tower, the bronze statue of William Penn stands magnificently watching over his city and its people.

Doc and Jack are walking through one of the stone gargoyled archways leading south, out of Philadelphia City Hall's inner court yard.

"Well, anyway that is how I feel Jack, I mean, I'm completely stumped on this one."

"I know, believe me I know, me too."

Doc relights his unlit cigar, as they walk. "You know when I was I little kid, I saw horror films that would answer some of these questions." As he looks at Jack with a smile, trying not to laugh, "And I'm not kidding."

Jack smiles, nodding his head, as they approach a group of cars illegally parked on the expansive exterior sidewalk of city hall. "I'm parked over here." Jack studies his friend. "Can I give you a lift Doc?"

"Well, how about getting something to eat? I'm starving." He looks at Jack and smiles, a quizzical smile, "We could go to a bar if you like?"

"You're on."

"But, lets drive there, okay Jack?" Taking a few puffs of his cigar, as he talks. "I'm tired of walking."

"Sure," Jack walks to his black car, which is sandwiched between the other illegally parked cars, beside a no parking sign. Jack unlocks the passenger door of his car, and then walks around to his door, as the Doc gets in to his car.

As Jack gets in, he tries to straighten up by crumpling up the empty beer cans lying on the floor of the car and putting them into the brown paper bag that was lying beside them.

"You should hide these beer cans better Jack."

"Yeah, I know," smiling, "good thing I can't get locked up easily."

"You better believe it, kiddo."

Jack turns the ignition key, and the sound of the motor roars as it starts. "How about Dirty Franks?"

"How about where they actually have some food Jack?"

Jack laughs as he says, "Oh, Okay." Then Jack drives away down Broad Street. "How about the Midtown Tavern."

"That's good, their foods good."

Moments later Inside the Midtown Tavern, they are seated at the bar. Jack is drinking Heineken bottles of beer, the Doc's doing the same, but the Doc's eating an entire meal, whereas Jack is just drinking.

"Umm, this is great," pushing money out toward the bartender. "Bring me another meatloaf diner buddy, okay?"

Taking a gnawed unlit cigar from his mouth as he talks, "You got it," starting to walk away, but stops, as the Doc asks.

"Jack you want one too?"

"No, that's okay Doc, I'll eat later, I like this one diner near where I'm staying."

"Just the one meal then, and some more rolls, okay."

Now the bartender walks away, "You got it."

They sit there, Doc eating, and Jack just drinking. While Doc's eyes are studying Jack quietly, hesitantly. "Jack, there is something else screwy about this whole thing. I've found some saliva, blood, and something else, semen, on some of the victims."

"Yeah."

"And, it's not human Jack. I don't know what the hell it is, but it's not human."

"I don't understand?"

"Neither do I," Doc resumes eating, "neither do I," but as he is eating, he is thinking of something else....

"What?"

"After I finish at city hall, I'm going over to the morgue tonight to check it out."

In a booth near them, but hidden because of the high backs of the booth, the back of a man's head is visible. The way he leans in to their conversation indicates that he is listening to them.

"Want a lift to the morgue?"

"No, but could you drop me back at city hall?"

"Sure," smiling affirmatively now, but intently watching Doc. "But, take your time, and finish you meal first." As Doc resumes eating the last of his dinner, the bartender returns with his second meatloaf dinner. Jack sits back, and watches the Doc eat, quietly amused.

Smiling good naturally at the Doc, "Your second meal I mean."

"What?" amused by Jacks interest, "I was hungry."

Later Jack drives north on Broad Street, toward city hall. Its clock tower illuminating the night sky, beneath the mighty statue of William Penn, who stands magnificently on the very top of this tower, looking out over his city.

Meanwhile another big black car is discreetly following Jack's car, as it works its way down Broad Street. Jack makes the mandatory right turn circling city hall, and then bears to the left as it rounds the corner. Through the light at Market Street, and then jumps the curb, and drives on to the extremely wide sidewalk surrounding the square monolithic stone city hall.

The big black car surreptitiously follows Jack's car, past Market Street, and unobtrusively parks on the opposite side of the street, from Jack's car, at the stone Masonic hall, beside its black wrought iron estate spiked fence.

Jack pulls up at city hall's north east tower entrance, and stops. "You sure," hesitantly, "you don't want me to wait for you Doc? I don't mind."

"No, no Jack," as he opens the car's door, "I'll get a cab, I have to find out what's going on here, there must be a mistake." They're being watched, from across the street, by someone inside the big black car.

Doc gets out of Jack's car, "I'll see you tomorrow Jack." Jack leans out the window now, as the Doc walks over to the tower's entrance, opens one of the doors, and starts to go in. Jack yells to the Doc through the opened car window.

"You sure Doc?" As the Doc slowly turns, the sound of a beer can top popping open is heard. The Doc is laughing now, as he is relighting his cigar.

Jack yells out again, "All right, but I'm going to wait out here anyway, just in case."

"Okay, but give me one of those damn things," as he's walking back to Jack's car. Jack takes a can of beer, from a brown paper bag, on the seat.

104

"Here you go," and tosses it to him, "good then I'll wait."

Doc catches it, and walks back towards the entrance to city hall, "Okay, thanks."

Jack backs his car up out of the way of the entrance, settles back in his chair, drinks his beer and waits for the Doc.

The Doc walks through the doors, and looks straight up into the vastness of city hall's north east tower, as the spiraling marble staircase clings to the marble walls, and disappears five floors above into the darkness, of the extremely high vaulted tower's ceiling.

Doc walks across the time worn terrazzo floor, and enters the building's hallway, through the glass lobby doors. As he enters Doc watches the policeman at the desk, who has stopped reading the Daily News, and looking up, says, "Oh, hi Doc, working late huh?"

"Yeah, hope I can get out soon, see yeah." Doc enters the opened elevator car, and walks out of sight as the doors close.

Doc exits the elevator, drinking his opened can of beer, and starts the walk down the enormously long, dimly lit hallway, almost disappearing into the darkness as he walks. Looking about apprehensively, suddenly stopping he turns, and looks into one of the shadowy, concealed, deeply recessed doorways.

Upon reaching his own deeply recessed, shadowy doorway, and with the use of his keys, he enters his office.

While Jack sits drinking his beer, watching the headlights flash past him out in the street, from the fast moving cars, driving around the square monolithic city hall structure. He tries to dismiss his deeply troubling thoughts, of the murdered children, as he drinks his beer.

While a deeply engrossed Doc sits at his desk, looking at his computer screens information, comparing the many other notes he has taken, during the months and months of autopsies he has performed on the skeletal remains of these murdered little girls and their mothers.

Intermittently rising to retrieve, heavy looking, large, thick, medical books, from a wall of books, and then examining detailed information from yet different large volumes, in his cluttered office.

A now exhausted looking Doc looks about his office, and then he hurriedly picks up the files on his desk, and puts them along with his notes into his brief case. He looks furtively about the room before he turns out the lights, and then exits out into the hallway.

At the same moment, Jack is standing beside his car, drinking his beer and watching the passing lights as the cars speed around the corner out in the street.

While from across the street, inside a big black car, Detective Johnson sits watching Jack standing beside his car, as Johnson's listening to country and western music on his little portable radio.

Meanwhile a distraught Doc, is hurriedly walking back through the long forebodingly dark hallways, of city hall's

106

imposing stone structure. Passing dozens, after dozens of pitch black doorways, which are set back several feet off of the hallway, adding to the illusion of danger. As he walks, he anxiously looks back over his shoulder, and peers into the darkness, with much apprehension, while his imagination is running wild, fearing all sorts of dangers, lurking in the shadows.

As he finally returns to the bank of elevator doors on one side, and the old wood glass panel doors leading to the stairwell tower on the other. He presses the elevator button on the wall, and waits, impatiently looking at his wristwatch, and then back up at the indicator lights above the bank of elevator doors, indicating the whereabouts of the elevator cars. Revealing that all the elevator cars are on the first floor, and have not even begun to move up yet.

An exasperated Doc looks through the wooden door's glass, into the darkness of the stairway's tower, and back to the elevators doors.

He hesitates, then hurriedly walks through the doors, and on to the fifth floor stairwell's landing. At the landings banister, he leans over the brass railing, and looks down into the dark vastness of the spiraling staircases clockwise descent into the void. Illuminated only by the moon light, entering through the single row of windows descending from mid-floor-landing to mid-floor-landing. A faint golden glint, reflects off of the brass railing as it snakes its way down onto the dimly lighted foyer far below.

Through one of the lower windows, Doc can see Jack standing outside of his black car. Doc reenters onto the fifth floor hallway, and again looks above the bank of elevator doors, at the indicator lights. Which show that all the elevator cars, are still on the first floor, an undecided Doc waits impatiently.

As Detective Johnson watches, from across the street, Jack standing beside his car, Johnson looks down for a moment to get another can of beer, pops the top and returns his gaze across the street, but now there is no Jack to be seen. Detective Johnson picks up a pair of binoculars to search, but although Jack's car is still there, he is nowhere to be seen.

A rattled Detective Johnson quickly gets out of his car, spilling some of his beer, and half runs across the street. Surreptitiously looking about as he reaches the other side of the streets extremely wide sidewalk, and darts quickly to the side of the building. Attempting to hide from Jack's sight if he is near, and then he visually searches the surrounding sidewalk for any sight of Jack, but there is no sign of Jack to be found.

Back on the fifth floor, Doc still waits impatiently, and then seeming to make up his mind, he quickly walks through the doors, to the stairway landing's railing, pausing momentarily, and then he starts to quickly walk down the steps.

As he walks, he leans over the railing, and looks down into the deep dark void below. While making his long decent into the darkened staircase, he passes a window, as he reaches the first mid floor landing. Where he stops beside the railing, to take a deep breath of air, before he looks up into, the pitch black darkness of the high vaulted ceiling above, and then gazes back down into the lower floors below.

Continuing to descend, and upon reaching the fourth floor landing, the Doc stops, takes a breath, and looks over the railing. Looking through a lower window, the Doc sees Jack's car but no Jack, but he sees something beside the window, in the shadows. There appears to be a darker than normal shadow, against the marble wall, he tries to discount this, as he apprehensively continues his descent, into the circular stairwells dark void.

While hidden within the extreme darkness of the stairwell, something is looking up. Seeing the Doc, in a kind of black & white tunnel vision, as the Doc is looking down from the upper reaches of the tower above. While the sounds of a heart beating, pounding is heard, as it is watching the Doc's descent into the darkness.

Upon reaching the next mid-floor-landing, Doc stops, catches his breath again, and then continues down the stairs, while leaning over the brass railing, and peering into the darkness to see the shadowy apparition, but this time, it seems to have moved further from the window.

Continuing to descend the Doc reaches the third floor landing, and he again glances below, leaning on to the railing beside him, and looking down, through a window below, he sees Jack's car, but still doesn't see Jack anymore. Then looking to the shadow, the Doc discovers that it is not there, it is GONE ...

... an instant later, a black shadow is being cast against the marble walls, seemingly flying up the staircase's steps hurdling towards the Doc. Hearing the sound of footsteps rapidly approaching up the staircase, Doc glances down into the darkness, and sees ...

... a shadowy, black robed, demonic looking apparition, racing up the steps below, its glowing yellow eyes, burning into his soul. A paralyzing fear over takes the Doc, and while still shaking with fear, he starts to run back up the steps, he just walked down.

Inside the foyer of city hall's stairwell now, Detective Johnson spots the shadowy demonic apparition, following Doc up into the towers darkness, and drawing his gun from his holster, he quickly follows the demonic apparition, up into the spiraling stairwell above.

The shadowy demon watches, in black and white, tunnel vision, the Doc frantically climbing the staircase, now only one floor from the demon.

The out of breath Doc stops, and looks back down, and he sees the terrifying demon gaining on him. In desperation as the Doc looks up, he sees he'll soon be running out of steps to climb, seeing the darkness of the upper staircase's vaulted ceiling. The demons quickly gaining on the Doc now, and will soon be on him, as the sound of a heart beating pounding is heard increasing in volume.

Detective Johnson continues to climb, as quickly and as quietly as he can, gun in hand, watching the shadowy demonic apparition, gaining ground on the Doc.

The Doc again returns to the fifth floor landing, and franticly runs through the old wooden glass doors, leading him back on to the fifth floor hallway, and the same elevator doors where he waited moments ago. He quickly looks to the indicator lights above the bank of elevator doors, and sees ...

... an elevator car is fast approaching the fifth floor. Doc looks back to the stairway landing's doors. He hears a chime, and turns to see the elevator doors opening. He looks quickly back to the landing's doors behind him, and as he dashes into the seemingly empty elevator car, something dark suddenly steps from the one side of the car onto the fifth floor bumping into the Doc rushing in....

... An extremely scared Doc screams ... it is the policeman from the lobby below, the startled policeman backs up suddenly, screaming …

"What the hell's going on?" The Doc quickly ushers the policeman back into the elevator car, as he shouts out …

"Hurry!" While being dragged back into the elevator car, the policeman again asks.

"What the hell's wrong?"

As the Doc drags him back into the elevator car, turning to look back the terrified Doc sees the wooden stairwell's doors starting to open. Just then the elevator doors suddenly close, and the elevator car starts to quickly descend, as seen on the lighted board beside the doors.

"I'll tell you when we're the hell out of here."

As an apprehensively cautious Detective Johnson, climbs the last few steps to the fifth floor landing. He looks around and walks, gun in hand to the hallway's doors. Suddenly the doors swing in, banging into him, knocking the gun out of his hand.

Through the door enters the black hooded demon. Seeing this demonic apparition, frightens the hell out of Detective Johnson, but he quickly evades the apparent demon, by escaping through the doors leading onto the fifth floor hallway, and sprints into the darkness. The hooded demon enters through the doors, and pursues the terrified Detective Johnson's flight down the long dark hallway.

A sprinting Detective Johnson looks back to see, the shadowy demon quickly gaining on him, its yellow eyes threateningly glaring back at him. As Detective Johnson reaches the end of the hallway, and disappears around the corner, he is running with a wild abandonment, down the adjoining hallway.

Half way down the adjoining hallway, he reaches doors on the right, leading onto yet another dark staircase, and before he enters these doors, he looks back to see, an empty hallway corridor, devoid of the demon. He pushes open the doors, and runs onto the stairway, and he starts down the steps, when suddenly from the darkness of the upper steps jumps, the shadowy demon, knocking Detective Johnson down, and in an instant, in the darkness the sounds of bones breaking are heard. The demons on top of Detective Johnson's limp body, and then a loud cracking sound is heard, as the demon breaks Johnson's neck, bending it grotesquely behind him.

While below, the elevator's doors open onto the lobby's hallway floor, and the Doc quickly exits the elevator car, followed by the unsettled policeman. Walking quickly toward the doors leading to the foyer, the Doc looks to his right, down the long hallway, then back to the foyer's doors, as the exasperated policeman yells, "What the hell's going on Doc?"

Doc pulls the policeman through the doors, and onto the stairway towers foyer. "I don't know how to say this," as the Doc looks up into the tower's pitch black spiraling stairwell, while quickly moving toward the exit, "but I think I was ..."

"Is everything okay?" The policeman asks, looking about, as he follows him, "Are you all right?"

"I don't know," looking back at the hallway doors, they just exited, "did anyone come in here just now? After me?"

"What the hell's going on?"

Looking around as he speaks, "Did you hear two sets of feet?"

"I don't know," approaching the Doc, "maybe? Maybe that's why I come up. What the hell is going on here?"

"I don't know ... what I saw," waving the officer away, "I need a drink. I'm going to go, Okay?"

"Sure Doc, if you're okay."

The Doc quickly walks away, but as he does he looks up into darkness of the tower's upper staircase, and fear quickly over takes him, as he hurries to the exterior doors, and swiftly exits. The policeman follows him outside.

"What the hell happened up there?"

"I don't know I," looking around as he speaks, "I think, I know this sounds crazy, but, I think I've just seen a ghost, up there," looking up at the windows of the stairwell's tower, "up there in the tower."

The policeman laughs, "Oh, is that all. Hell, I see them all the time up there." The policeman continues laughing, as he walks away, "Take care Doc," and he goes back through the doors onto the towers foyer again.

A clearly shaken Doc, watches the retreating policeman, and then hurries to Jack's car, takes his flask of whiskey from his coat pocket, and drinks a long belt. Glancing back at the stairway tower doors as he does so, and then he enters Jack's car. The Doc quickly locks Jack's car doors, as he sits apprehensively, and as he waits he drinks, first his whiskey then Jack's beer.

The sound of the car's trunk opening suddenly, startles the Doc, and it then slams shuts. Then the driver door opens, and Jack enters the car.

Doc looks nervously at Jack, "Where were you?" Jack looks at the Doc, but then he looks back at the building's entrance again, he is thinking of something. Doc asks, "What?"

As Jack gets back out, he says, "I'll be right back." Jack then reenters the building....

Doc's fearful glances betray his attempt at bravado. He finishes drinking a can of beer, and then while opening another, Doc nervously looks back at the gargoyled building, while the passing car's headlights out in the street, flash past him.

Again the sudden sound of the car's trunk opening, startles the Doc, and then it slams shut again as Jack reenters the car, and he says, "Okay let's go."

Later, In the distance, the city morgue's loading dock comes into view. Jack looks to the Doc as he pulls up to the rear loading dock's gated entrance. "Want some company Doc?"

"No, no you go get some sleep Jack, I'll call you, tomorrow." Doc gets out and walks along the side walk leading to the morgue.

As Jack watches the Doc walking away, approaching the entrance of the morgue, he yells out.

"See you Doc."

The Doc yells, "I'm okay now, I'll call you tomorrow Jack."

Waving to the Doc as he starts to leave, "Okay, see you." Jack then drives down the dark street, leaving the morgue in the distance.

CHAPTER 21

Later that night, Jack walks across Vine Street, and climbs the numerous steps of the Philadelphia Logan Circle Library's main entrance. Note pads under his arm, and carrying three large cups of coffee, while glancing at his notes. He looks up to see a sharply dressed, young black girl, coming down the steps. She walks right beside him, stops, looks dead at Jack, and flashes a gorgeous knowing smile at him, and says, "Hi Jack." She then lowers her gaze, turns away, and walks past him down the steps.

A speechless Jack turns, thinking who is she, while watching her every move as she walks down the steps, on to the sidewalk and away down the street without looking back. Looking puzzled, he turns to watch her once more, and then continues walking up the steps.

Jack enters the library, walks across the vast open foyer, up the marble steps at the far end of the room, and on to the landing. Where the stairway splits in two, he continues walking choosing the stairway rising off to the right. As he climbs, he seems to disappear climbing into an even higher ceiling, opening on to an enormous vaulted ornately plastered ceiling.

Looking over a marble balustrade onto the main floor below, Jack walks into view from the left, coming up one of the two matching stairways, continuing to slide his hand along the banister, as he climbs the deep marble stair treads. Continuing to walk along, and entering on to the enormous hallway, and walks down the very wide hallway into one of the many high vaulted reading rooms.

Inside one of the enormous reading rooms, Jack appears from behind a row of book cases, carrying a small mountain of very large reference books. He proceeds to walk, beside the third floor black iron railing, to one of the two circular spiraling black wrought iron staircases, and descends the three floors of steps. Upon reaching the main floor again he walks over to a large table where he was apparently sitting before, because his notebooks and coffee cups are there, and sitting down begins to read one of the large books.

Later Jack sits at a viewer, watching old newspaper headlines, on microfilm. Reading the news of long ago, and writing down pertinent information as he reads, while empty coffee containers, opened notebooks, and scattered papers, litter the table.

And as time passes, Jack is again talking to the librarian, at the film department, as the librarian walks away, Jack is looking down at a note pad, he has written on. The librarian returns and hands him boxes of microfilm. Jack returns to his viewer, and starts to reload the machine.

Still later as Jack sits quietly staring at the floor, a look of utter defeat creeps on to his face, shaking his head in disgust, he then gathers up his notes, and dumps them all into a nearby waste paper basket.

A dejected Jack absentmindedly exits the Library, through one of the many exterior doors, he walks down the steps, out onto and across the street, and down the block to where his car is illegally parked. He opens the door, and suddenly looks around, thinking he saw some shadowy figure following him move in the dark.

Still later that night, from the darkness of the morgue's hallway, looking through the partially opened doors, past the rows of empty gurneys, where the latest sheet covered victims lie. The Doc is examining one of the brutalized bodies. Now he is taking samples of the victim's blood, and skin tissue samples. Placing them on to sterile glass microscope's slides, carrying them to a long wall of glass fronted sterile looking stainless steel medical cabinets hanging above the numerous stainless steel sinks and base cabinets. Where the Doc is examining these samples under a microscope, and writing something into his note book.

In another one of the Doc's large offices, at the morgue, the Doc takes a very large reference book down from the wall of book cases, and begins to read. While something is watching the Doc, moving slowly closer, step by step, as the Doc is completely engrossed, working on his notes. Reexamining the blood, and tissue samples, that he has previously taken, under the microscope again, completely baffled, and silently mumbling to himself, "This can't be, this is impossible, it doesn't make any sense."

CHAPTER 22

Pete's Place is empty, except for Jack, and Charlie who is leaning on the bar across from Jack. They are drinking Heinekens and Irish whiskey, and talking quietly. Charlie is pounding back another double, and filling the glasses of his friend Jack, and himself, as the front door opens, and a beautiful, young, sexy Oriental prostitute, enters the bar. They turn as they hear the sound of her high heels tapping onto the old hard wood floor. She smiles at the boys as she walks toward the ladies' room, which is passed the bar and to the right.

Charlie and Jack watch her every move, and as the ladies room door closes, Charlie rolls his eyes, and Jack smiles at long last. The two whisper to each other, as they drink their Heinekens, and share a quiet laugh together.

When she reappears, she sits down next to Jack, puts her tiny bright red purse on her lap, opens it, takes out some money, and puts it on the bar. Crossing her black silk stockinged legs, she fiddles with a delicate gold ankle bracelet, removes one of her bright red shoes, rubs her tiny foot, smiles, and slyly eyes Jack's change from a fifty, sitting on the bar, by his drinks.

Smiling seductively, "I'd like a Smirnoff Ice."

"We don't have that, but how about a cold beer?" Smiling as she shakes her head no, she puts her shoe back on, opens her purse and puts her money from the bar away. She also takes out a small make up case, and watching herself in its tiny mirror, starts to invitingly reapply a bright red lip stick to her lips.

121

She gets up, and as she walks away slides her long blood red finger nails gently along Jack's hair, and neck. She then turns back, and smiles to them both.

"Bye boys, maybe some other night." And then she walks sultrily out of the bar. They watch transfixed as she leaves, slowly shaking their heads.

"You should stock that stuff Charlie."

"Now you tell me."

Later that night, elevated trains are heard rumbling above Kensington Avenue, throwing quick moving lights upon the buildings and everything else. While creating strange shadows, cast down on to the street below. As the steel beams supporting the tracks above, line the street below, like weird rows of steel trees creating even more dangerous shadows, and places to hide behind, or suddenly surprise, and attack some unsuspecting person walking fearfully in and out of the darkness.

Jack is driving slowly, under the elevated train track above, along Kensington Avenue. Looking at the many prostitutes who sell their wares along the avenues steel columned shadowy street corners. From the darkened shadows a young Spanish prostitute stepping into the light, is beckoning to Jack to pull over at the corner. Jack looks long and hard at the young girl's long legs, and near naked attire. The beautiful brunet is dressed to kill. Jack looks like he is going to stop, but then he drives off.

The Oriental prostitute from earlier in the evening, is standing on a corner, not far from Pete's bar, under the elevated train's tracks. She suddenly ducks into the darkness, as a police car slows down, but doesn't stop, and then it drives on down the street. She watches the police car disappear into the darkness of the night, and then she emerges from the shadows again.

While watching in black and white tunnel vision, and driving a big black car, someone or something is quickly approaching the Oriental prostitute up at the next corner, as the sound of a heart beating, pounding and heavy breathing like a wolf is heard.

The young prostitute is shrouded in darkness, as the big black car moves slowly down the street, drawing closer to the young girl. She sees its approach, as It stops beside her, the window comes down.

She suddenly smiles, and says, "Oh it's you," as the car's door opens, and she gets in. The big black car speeds away, seemingly disappearing into the darkness of the night.

A big black car is driving north along the East River Drive, while on the other side of the Schuylkill River, the lights of the Philadelphia Zoo illuminate the night sky. The snake like curving road, cuts through the rock tunnel beneath Amtrak's railroad tracks above.

The car turns on to a smaller road, jumps the curb, drives down the hill, out of the view from the road, and pulls up into the woods as close as it can get to the crime scene of the other night, where the skeletal remains were found.

Jack gloomily thinks to himself ...

"Thousands of people, teenagers, children disappear every day, they never come home again, they're never seen again, and they're never found."

Jack gets out of his black car, taking his opened beer with him, and stands there in what seems an eternity, before he goes into the woods. Jack thinks he sees something move, as he finishes his beer, and walks back to his car, unlocks the trunk, and reaches in for something. Suddenly he sticks up his head quickly, and then cautiously looks around, before reaching into the truck of the car to extract something unseen from the trunk.

The woods surrounding the desolate spot are extremely dark, as the sound of a trunk lid slamming shut, pierces the silence of the woods. A shadow moves furtively along the grassy ground, cast there by the moon's intensity.

The obscure shadow is moving slowly, walking deeper into the woods, its muddy shoes are walking slowly into the woods, splashing through the murky water, leaving deep foot prints as it walks, down the grassy hill, back into the woods.

Later Jack is walking back out of the woods, there is something dark on his hands, clothes, and shoes. He is carrying a beer, drinking as he walks, softly mumbling something to himself.

Back at Jack's flop house, Jack is taking a shower in an ill lit, seedy, grimy shower stall. An opened can of beer sits on the mildewed soap tray. On the floor of the shower, running into the drain, is a dark substance, in the dark it is hard to make out what it is.

Still later Jack is sleeping restlessly, mumbling something incoherently as he dreams ...

... Of looking down a dark fogy alley, as he walks, everything is hazy. He cautiously walks past a couple of black guys shooting craps at the corner's curb. They look up at him and motion to their right, down the cross street. Everything is out of proportion, the building's angles are out of kilter leaning way to one side.

As Jack turns the corner, there is the leggy black girl from the library steps, looking up the block, leaning against a pole. She is scantily dressed, almost naked, resembling a prostitute. Jack looks off, toward where she is looking ...

... And, when he looks back, there is a black Panther there instead, and the Panther is looking right at him. Growling softly, and starting to growl loudly exposing her large fangs ...

... Awakening with a start, Jack bolts upright in bed, and tries to quiet his racing heart.

*   *   *

While at the same moment, a concerned Sheila is looking into Nicole's bedroom, who is asleep in a cozy, love filled room of toys, and stuffed animals to watch over and protect her.

Sheila is watching Nicole while she is sleeping, and walking quietly into the bedroom she sits in a chair beside her restlessly sleeping daughter. Nervously watching over her, and tiring over time, she slowly falls asleep, while her little Nicole is beginning to have another nightmare ...

... The dream is in black and white, foggy, and hard to see several feet past the edges of the bed, which is slowly spinning around in circles, like a top. As headless corpses are walking around the bed. Their bodies are

125

blackened greenish brown, and their clothes are rotting off their decomposing bodies. Brown red clotted blood is leaking off their severed throats, as they walk around the bed. While a continuous frightening melodious chant, in an ancient, almost extinct language, is continuing throughout the entire dream.

In the fog the bed seems to be lifting slightly, as Nicole is sitting up, trying to scream, but nothing's coming out. The encircling headless corpses part, as a purple black hooded, monk like robed demon is walking toward her out of the shadows, its face unseen but for its glowing yellow eyes, as it voraciously approaches her …

… Nicole wakes up screaming, "Aaaaaaahhhhhhh help me, help me, mommy ..."

CHAPTER 23

In the darkness of early morning, the sound of a bell, as if far off in the distance, is heard clanging, as a hand is fumbling for a clock on the night stand, knocking it onto the floor, suddenly stopping the clanging of the clock.

Jack's hand moves up to his head, wearily rubbing his eyes, and forehead. Then rolling out of bed and looking around the room, Jack sees beer cans littering the room, and a whiskey bottle lying on its side. Picking up the whiskey bottle, he tries to get one more drink, but it is empty. He then looks about the room for something to drink, and gives up. He reaches for his pants, and his muddy shoes, as he stumbles toward the door.

Jack unlocks the door of his room, and walks down the hallway, past the stairway's railing, other locked doors, and heads into the floors bathroom. Behind the bathroom door is the sound of running water, and someone being sick in the bathroom.

*   *   *

Dawn is breaking over this sleepy little mountain ringed town, in upstate Pennsylvania, as Nicole sits at the kitchen table, rubbing her eyes with the palms of her little hands, as she tries to wake up.

Sheila is cooking breakfast, and looks up to see her other two children, Carol and Heather as they sleepily enter the kitchen, and they join their sister at the table. Later the girls get up and help their mother set the table.

Sheila brings a plate of bacon, and eggs for Nicole, and sets it before her. The other children are already eating quietly. "Here you are sweetie, eat it before it gets cold." The small child smiles at her mother, and starts to eat quietly.

"Thank you mommy." Sheila kisses her head, then gets her coffee, and sits down to eat.

Later at the front door, Sheila kisses her children goodbye, and then watches them walk away down the street, headed off to school.

*   *   *

Jack is walking though one of the many recent crime scenes, trying to establish what happened, how it happened, and what is more important, why it happened, and why, the way it happened. Thinking to himself as he examines the surrounding area.

"Was it premeditated, or was it spontaneous," he asks himself. "There were no shoe prints found because of the thick underbrush, and in the surrounding woods there were no signs of anything out of the usual." After searching through every possible clue, real or imagined. Jack is heading up the hill, proceeding to walk out of the park, through the thick woods. He is deep in thought, talking to himself as he walks …

"Crazy as it sounds, but I feel like someone is watching me, walk through the woods, like someone is following me all the time, I know it sounds nuts, but that's how I feel."

Jack walks to his car, and looks around suddenly. Seeing nothing, he gets into his car, and drives away down the dirt path leading to the entrance to the road.

CHAPTER 24

Little children are playing on the merry-go-round, swings, and slides. Their smiling mothers are standing around watching them absentmindedly, enjoying their moments in the sun. Three little children are playing together on the merry-go-round, enjoying themselves, not aware of anything, but their happiness, engulfed in their own innocence. They are Sheila's kids, their happy the way children should be, but so often are not.

Someone, or something is watching them, in a sort of black and white tunnel vision, while walking down the tree lined sidewalk, beside the playgrounds black wrought iron spiked fence. The sound of a heart beating loudly is heard, while watching them, through the spaces between the iron bars, as it walks toward the young girls, who are happily playing on the merry-go-round, one hundred feet ahead, and on other side of the fence.

The sound of a walking stick being dragged along the fence's iron bars is heard, tapping ... Tap ... Tap ... Tap ... Tap ... Tap ... as the walking stick is continuing to being dragged along the iron spiked fence. The view of Sheila's children, between the black Iron bars, is becoming closer and closer. The sound of the tapping awakens the attention of one of Sheila's children, who are still busy playing ...

... It is Sheila's little child Nicole, but no one else seems to notice the tapping sound ...

Nicole is looking to where the strange tapping sounds are coming from, while on the merry-go-round, spinning around in circles, trying to see what is making the sound of the tapping.

While his walking stick is being dragged along the iron spiked fence, he is looking between the iron bars of the fence, at Nicole on the spinning merry-go-round. Stopping beside the children, who are fifty feet away on the opposite side of the black iron barred fence, while watching Nicole as she is happily playing. His extremely powerful hands are now grasping the iron bars. He is wearing an unusually large ornate platinum ring, inlaid with precious jewels of an unusual ancient design, on the smallest finger of his large hairy right hand.

Nicole is becoming dizzy from spinning on the merry-go-round, it distorts her vision, as she is going around in circles, trying to grasp where she is ...

Watching from between the iron bars, Nicole has now gotten off the ride, and is staring at him. His right hand relaxes his grip on one of the iron bars, and extending his manicured hand through the bars, he beckons her to come to him, with his extended index finger, and she starts to approach him ...

Just then Sheila calls to her children, "Nicole, Heather, Carol, let's go. Come on children, it's time to go."

The two older children quit playing on the merry-go-round, and start to run to their mother, but Nicole is still staring off in the other direction, and she is walking toward him, slowly like in a trance.

Sheila approaches her and looks in the direction of her child's gaze, and sees nothing ...

There is no one there, no one except a very large ferocious looking black dog, which is looking through the iron fence's bars. Its strangely yellow eyes, are burning brightly, as the sound of menacing growling is heard.

Nicole has stopped walking toward the fence, and is now standing there looking transfixed at it, as if in a hypnotized state.

Watching the little girl looking directly at him. The sound of growling and heavy breathing is heard, over the sound of a loudly beating heart. As his powerful hands continue to grip the iron bars, it seems as if the iron bars are being pulled apart.

Nicole watches the black dog's red tongue licking its fangs, as its head is sticking through a wide gap in the fence, where the iron bars have been pulled apart, but its very wide shoulders are unable to get between, and through the fence's iron bars.

A frightened Sheila snatches Nicole up in her arms, while Nicole is still looking off in the same direction as before, and carrying her hurries off in the opposite direction, toward the open gate leading to her parked car, off on the parking lot. Sheila's other two children have already begun to run off in that direction, and are approaching the gate, while Nicole continues to look back over her mother's shoulder…

It is still watching between the iron bars, watching Nicole, as her mother hurriedly carries her away, through the gate, and to her car.

Hustling her children into her car, while looking around and back at the playground, then hastily getting into her car and driving away. Nicole is still looking back, as the car is speeding away.

CHAPTER 25

As dawn is breaking, off in the distance, Jack is looking into the mirror of his boarding house's bathroom, shaving quietly, with a forlorn expression on his exhausted face. There is a determined atmosphere about the way he is looking into the steam covered mirror. Almost as if he was trying to hide from his own recognition of himself, as if to methodically deny his own existence, afraid to face something, he apparently has to do.

Back in his room, he is getting dressed, although this melancholy pervades everything Jack does, even to reexamining his gun to be sure it is fully loaded before slipping it into his shoulder holster.

As he looks into the old dresser's mirror, his depressed expression reflecting back, Jack wonders to himself, who this strange man really is looking back at him, before he slips on his suit jacket, and adjusts his black tie. Exiting his meager boarding house's bedroom, into the hallway, and after locking his door, he trudges down the dark hallway toward the stairway.

Later while Jack is driving west on Girard Avenue, and as he is snaking his way through the city streets until the morgue comes into view, his mind is far from the present, still lingering in the past, as he drives into the parking lot. He parks, gets out and is walking along the sidewalk, beside the fence leading toward the morgue's loading docks entrance, and is thinking out loud as he walks …

... "I was trying to remember what he said to me, the last time I saw him," while walking up the steps beside the loading dock, and entering the back door, like he has done a hundred times before.

"The little girl had been ripped apart, brutally murdered, and Doc said something to me, I forget somehow, I don't know. I couldn't make any sense of it, but then Doc asked me, 'if I realized what it could possibly mean, if I saw it,' and I said I didn't." As Jack waves to the policeman behind the glass wall, the buzzer sounds, and lets him in to the hallway.

"He said, 'Call me tomorrow Jack,' and I said Okay." As Jack walks down the hallway, into the empty waiting elevator, and the doors close behind him.

"Tomorrow proved to be too late. Doc was found dead on his boat. His boat was still tied up at his dock site, on the Delaware River. He'd been missing work for several days." The elevator doors open, on to the morgue's dark basement hallway, almost pitch black, except for the occasional low hanging lights.

As Jack is walking through the opened elevator doors, he seems to almost disappear, as he is walking into the darkness, then is seen again while under a low hanging light, and is then thrust back into the darkness again, as the long foreboding hallway leads a hesitant Jack towards the morgue's operating theater.

Jack resumes his inner thoughts ... "But, his car was still in his driveway, back at his home, so how did he get there, to his boat, if he didn't drive. It's twenty miles from his house to the boat. Late that night, I forgot what he'd even told me, but he was found ripped to pieces."

At the end of the hallway, Jack pushes open one of a pair of extremely wide stainless steel doors, and walks into the operating theater. Past the empty gurneys, seventy feet or more, to the refrigerated bank of drawers containing all the murdered bodies, including oddly enough, the drawer with the Doc's own sheet covered body.

Jack hesitates a while, holding the handle, unable to cope with his friend's death, before he pulls open the drawer with the dead body of his best friend in the whole world, the Doc.

Jack stands there a long time, looking down at his sheet covered friend, finally pulling back the sheet exposing the Doc's battered, and unrecognizable face.

"Doc tried to get in touch with me the night he died. I know because Charlie said he'd called. Charlie said he told the Doc he'd give me the message, but the Doc said he'd call back later." Jack wipes away the tears from his eyes, "but he didn't ..."

Then Jack walks over and opens the drawer containing the latest dead child, but he can't bring himself to uncover her, standing there watching her sheet covered little body, he can't find the strength to look at her.

"I went to the morgue, to say goodbye to Doc, and look in on my last case. She was still there, poor little thing, maybe 3 or 4 years old. Laid out for us to see, her little brutalized body, skull crushed, and she'd been gnawed on by an animal, but that wasn't the only thing, her heart had been removed surgically. That's what Doc's notes revealed, maybe that's what he wanted to tell me, but now I'll never know" Jack closes the drawer, unable to look at her.

He then returns to his friend ... Jack stands there silently watching him. Finally, unable to bear the pain anymore, he leans over, and kisses his friends battered forehead, and then says a quiet prayer, beside the Doc. Then he covers up his friend, closes his drawer, and walks to the exiting doors.

Stopping and looking around in a strangely almost final farewell sort of way, he then turns, and walks through the wide stainless steel doors, and out into the almost pitch black hallway.

Walking back into the darkness, beneath the occasional light, and then thrust back into the dark, with its deathly smell pervading every corner.

"I went home that evening, determined to never go back to work ever again ..."

CHAPTER 26

Later that night, a despondent very morose Jack, sits at the bar talking to his now only friend in the world, the night bar tender Charlie. They are alone in Pete's Place, drinking at the bar.

"Look, I'm not saying what the Doc said, isn't true." Charlie says as he leans in, and looks about him, with much apprehension.

"But look at it this way, he might think that he's," Charlie stops talking, and gets them both another beer. "A demon or something," looking intently at Jack at this point, "in his mind I mean, see what I mean?"

"What a minute, you mean a guy who's nuts?"

"Exactly," pouring out more whiskey, "so why don't you talk to a shrink?"

Jack watches Charlie intently, as he almost whispers out, "You know what Charlie, maybe your right."

"Well, anyway this ones on me," Charlie raises his glass, "salute."

Jack drinks his whiskey, and then sits staring at his now empty glass, as a long pause ensues …

"You know Charlie, I don't remember where I was, or did, or what happened to me last night," as Charlie refills their glasses, "or any night anymore," picking up his now full drink. "I wake up, and don't know where I was, or what I did …"

Charlie pauses, and then he says …

…"Maybe that's a blessing," they both laugh, "knowing you as I do." Lifting their glasses, "Salute."

That night as Jack sleeps, we see his bedroom is covered with his notes, the photos of the crime scene, his folders from his office, and his notes from the past few days. Empty beer cans are on the desk, on the night table, and on the floor, a whiskey bottle beside his shoes.

Jack sleeps fitfully, on the bed fully clothed, murmuring something under his breath, moving his body as he mumbles, and he is clinching his fists open and closed, as his movements are getting more animated, with more jerking movements, he is dreaming and ...

... In his dream, he is in his car driving down a dark river road, there is no street lights, and there are no lights along the road of any kind. No houses, no cars, nothing, just shadows, images of surrealistic shadows reaching out to Jack from the trees.

While he is driving through an extremely dangerous section of this wooded curving road, and while staring at the road ahead, an extreme feeling of foreboding evil over comes Jack, as he furtively looks about. Jack happens to look into his rear view mirror, and sees ...

... a hooded, purple black robed demonic apparition looking back at him, and from within the darkness of the hood, two yellow eyes are glaring back. As he looks back to the road ahead, a shaken Jack tries to recover before the car swerves off the road.

In the distance, a mist moves on to the road ahead. It should be white or gray but it isn't, it is black, and he cannot see into it. Jack starts to weave along the road. Suddenly there is someone in the middle of the road, in the black fog, a little girl is in the middle of the road ahead, looking at Jack, and she is crying.

It is then that Jack realizes it is his missing child Nicole, looking straight at him, all bloody and dead looking.

Jack turns the wheel suddenly, and the sound of the screeching of brakes is heard, as a powerful pair of hands grabs Jacks throat, and on the demon's right hand, is a large ring, with an ancient design embedded with precious gems in its design. Jack turns his head, revealing a fearful look on his face, exposing his utter fright as he screams horrifically ...

... Then bolts up in bed, shivering in the dark, still seeing the road in front of him, and then the ghoulish apparition is gone, along with the black mist.

His hand shaking as he reaches out to put on a lamp, by his side, but before the darkness fades, he sees something, a deep purple black colored, peak hooded, extremely long sleeved figure, move in the dark, and then it to is gone! Jack rubs his eyes with the palms of his hands, as he stares at the blank wall. Then he lays back down, and tries to go back to sleep, but he forgets to turn out the light ...

... Or maybe he didn't forget.

*   *   *

While at the same moment upstate, in the midst of an impending storm, on a now familiar street, at Sheila's home, the sound of thunder suddenly loudly cracks, as the threatening storms lightning strikes nearby. Creating moving towering shadows cast against the house, by the lightning's brightness, thrust against the gusty wind tossed trees.

The howling storms winds, cause the tree's limbs to scrape eerily against the window panes of her house. Just as more bursts of thunder are heard, and torrential rains beat suddenly against the house.

In Nicole's bedroom, she sleeps fretfully, tossing back and forth, and looking as if she was fending of something, her arms flailing at some unseen horror. While Sheila is sleeping restlessly beside her troubled daughter, but the bed seems to be trembling, and then to be lifting slightly into the air, rocking back and forth slowly.

Then Nicole suddenly sits up in bed, staring straight ahead of her as she is obviously having a nightmare ...

... she is back at the playground, playing with her sisters, on a small spinning merry-go-round, and her vision is of one on a swirling ride ...

... As the sound of tapping off by the iron spiked fence, by the street, reveals in continuing flashes, a silver tipped cane being dragged along the cast iron spokes of the fence ...

... While viewing in black & white as if through a foggy tunnel, she is seeing herself through the eyes of someone walking towards her, and looking at herself now, through the gaps between the iron bars of the estate fence. While the sound of heavy breathing like an animal is heard, not a human sound, more like a wolf's breathing instead, panting alternating between growls, softly but clearly audible ...

Sheila who has been sleeping beside Nicole, on her child's bed wakes up with a jolt, feeling the bed, and her back. Something under the beds bedding is thrusting up,

146

as if a fist were punching up from the bed. A now standing Sheila is holding her trembling screaming child, as she is kissing her, and gently trying to get her to wake up,

"Wake up baby ... it's a dream ... it's a dream ..."

... A still dreaming Nicole is screaming. "Mommy, mommy help me, help me, I don't want to ... I don't want to ..."

CHAPTER 27

As the sun's first light slowly begins to gather over the skyline, breaking through the last remnants of last night's storm, and begins to rise, the sounds of birds chattering, to one another are heard.

Nicole is seeing her hand holding her mother's hand while walking with her mother, as she quickly sees the hole in the estate fencing, which she uses to exit the cemetery, in her short cut to her school. While across the street lies Saint Laurentius Catholic Church, with its well-manicured lawn, and flower garden. Where the good looking young man, from the other day, again toils spreading mulch in, and around the flower beds.

Nicole's view wanders from the street, to the curb, and back to looking across the street again, now seeing the young man intently, as he is continuing to work unaware that someone is watching him. She sees her mother, who is also intently watching the hard working young man. The young man slowly becomes aware of something, and looks up, and sees high heeled shoes walking slowly toward him, down the side walk. He then slowly looks up her shapely legs, and then on up her body, until he is now looking up at Sheila's lovely smiling face. She is looking directly at him, and then quickly looks down away from him ...

Sheila then looks back at him slowly, and smiles a dazzling smile. Sheila has stopped walking now, and has not started to leave, but is continuing to watch the young man. The young man picks a lovely flower, rises to his feet, walks to them, then kneels down, and offers the flower to Nicole, "Would you like a flower?"

Nicole's little hand comes into view as she reaches for the flower, and she says, "Thank you."

Mark says, "Your welcome," but he is clearly uneasy, as he can't help staring at Sheila. Who is staring back, and not in a shy way.

Nicole hears her mother say, "Come on dear we'll be late for your class..."

… Nicole's little hand waves good bye...

*   *   *

A loudly buzzing fly is trapped between, the opened double hung window sash, which is one of a row of windows, in Nicole's school room, and its buzzing sound attracts Nicole's attention.

We are watching the back of Nicole's head, as she is seated at her desk, looking out of the windows beside her on the left, as hairy clawed hands come into view. They are almost upon her when Nicole suddenly turns, sensing some danger lurking behind her, her frightened eyes widen as she turns, to see what is behind her, horrified she screams ...

... and then suddenly laughs uncontrollably...

She has fake whiskers, drawn in eye brow pencil, on her rosy cheeks like a cat. She is dressed all in black and has a large black tail like a cat, which freely moves about when she turns.

A look at the monster reveals it is a little child dressed up like a werewolf, looking around the classroom we see monsters all over the place ...

... enjoying a Halloween party at her schoolroom.

150

*   *   *

While Sheila and her neighbor Audrey, are sitting talking in her kitchen, Sheila is clearly very frightened.

"I came into my daughter's bedroom last night. I fell asleep while sitting there, and I felt, believe me, I felt something hit me from under her bed."

"What do you mean?"

"Like something was pushing or lightly punching me while I and Nicole slept. Nicole was having another nightmare at the time."

"Maybe you should go see a priest."

"Hum ... Maybe I should."

Sheila sits quietly looking at Audrey, and then down at the ground, while a quiet moment ensues ...

Later that afternoon, Sheila is looking into a large mirror in her bathroom, trying not to cry, but her eyes start to well up, and she starts to quietly cry.

As Jack is driving up to Sheila's house, he gets out noticing her house is decorated for Halloween, with gigantic black spiders clinging to cobwebs draped down from the tree tops, menacingly awaiting their dinner.

Walking home from her school's Halloween party, a happy Nicole still dressed in her cat outfit, ducks though the breach, in the iron spiked fence, and squeezes into Palmer Cemetery, for her short cut home. She is happily scampering along the cemeteries grass trodden, winding path leading home. When she comes upon the large black alley cat of the other day, but this time it is purring as Nicole approaches, and soon she is petting the large black cat, like it was a kitten of her own. Picking it up and

151

carrying the large black alley cat over her shoulder as she walks. Its hind paws dragging along the ground in front of her, its fore paws dragging along behind her as she walks. Struggling with the apparent weight of the black cat, and her school books.

Jack is sitting, at the kitchen table and Sheila is cooking dinner. "She'll be home in a few minutes now," smiling, "she's always late," Jack smiles, while listening quietly.

Nicole is still carrying the large alley cat as she walks up the back steps, leading into the kitchen. Nicole quickly enters, carrying the alley cat. An excitedly happy Nicole screams, "Mommy, mommy look what I found in the park, a kitten!" Jack and Sheila turn as she enters.

"Wait, stay there honey, that's it." As Sheila approaches her daughter, the black cat bristles at her, and hisses. Its hair stands up on its back, as it is still strung over the little girl's shoulder, struggling to get free. Sheila tries to pick it up, but the alley cat rears up on its hind legs, and hisses, as Nicole holds it to her, Sheila backs away from the alley cat.

"Honey put the cat down, back away from it."
"But, why?"
"Do as I say, now put it down, now!" Nicole puts the large alley cat down on the floor ...
"Now back away from it."
Sheila tries to scare the alley cat with a broom, but the large alley cat only stands its ground and growls back in defiance. Jack tries to get involved but Nicole steps in between. Now crying ...
"Don't hurt my kitten, Uncle Jack. I'll take it out," Nicole runs out of the kitchen, followed by the large cat. "Come on kitty, kitty, kitty, follow me."
Sheila watches her run out of the kitchen, then looks to Jack, as the sound of the house's front door

152

opening is heard, and then the screen door slamming shut.

Sheila follows her child, through into the other end of the house, and once again the front door is heard to open and then it slamming shut.

Later Sheila and her three children are sitting quietly as they eat. While Jack sits drinking a bottle of beer, his empty plate in front of him, watching them with a smile, as they finish their diner.

Still later, Nicole is happily running around the house in her cat costume, eagerly awaiting Halloween, so are her two sisters Carol and Heather. Who are also dressed up as black cats. While Jack and Sheila are sitting in the living room happily watching them ransack the house.

CHAPTER 28

The police precinct is still controlled chaos, as uniformed policemen go about their duties, while upstairs behind the Homicide Division's gold leafed glass door, Detective Thompson looks concerned at an angry Captain Shaw, who is clearly inflamed,

An exasperated Detective Thompson is talking to Captain Shaw.

"But it's been only what a couple days? Maybe he's drunk, he's gone missing before you know."

"Yeah, but his damned car got towed, across from city hall. Now go out and find Detective Johnson, you got that!"

"Yeah I got that."

"Good," standing up intimidatingly, "then get the HELL out, and find some damn thing."

*   *   *

As the full moon's pale, eerily moody light breaks through the extensive cloud cover, and casts long spooky shadows onto the landscape of a trash filled vacant lot. A ragged, skinny, hungry looking dog is rooting around in a pile of trash. While an old homeless man, is pushing a shopping cart, over flowing with large torn plastic trash bags, down the narrow rat infested alley.

"Ged out ah deah boy." The dog finds, and is dragging a shoe out from behind an old rusty steel barrel. The ferreting skinny dog rips the shoe free from the pile of trash, exposing a man's bloody foot.

"What youse got daah ... hum," examining this shoe, and then rummaging through the trash pile, as large rats scurry away from the site, the homeless man finds another shoe on the other foot of the dead man ...

"Hum, new shoes."

The old homeless man moves some more trash, and it exposes a man savagely beaten to death, horrifically battered black and blue. His swollen decaying and rat chewed head, almost unrecognizable.

The old homeless man lifts the dead man's wallet from a blood soaked pocket, and inside finds a detective's gold shield.

"Humm ... Detective Johnson," he takes out the money. "He ain't gonna need dis."

He puts the money into his sock, and puts the wallet back. It is clearly the body of Detective Johnson, as the old homeless man removes Detective Johnson's other shoe, and sits down to try them on.

Smiling happily, while looking down at his new shoes... "Humm ... nice shoes," still looking at his new shoes, "come on boy." The dog happily follows him, as he pushes his shopping cart, full of all his worldly goods, down the alley with a new air of success.

*   *   *

Jack is alone in his room, reading at the desk, which is covered with his old notes, photos of the crime scenes, and his notes from the past few days, drinking a can of beer as he writes out his ideas, thinking out loud as he writes ...

"There's no link between one murdered child or another, no connection between the victims at all, except that they've all been killed in what appears to be the same way, but why? ... Why were they killed at all, there has to be a reason, there has to be a link?"

Jack returns to looking through more of the files, as he mumbles to himself. "I've checked all the resent newspaper clipping from the area. Also into the past few years, and there was nothing to be learned from it, and what about Doc, who killed him? The same person, and if so why?"

After working almost all night a tired Jack falls asleep, head on his arms at the desk, still holding his beer can. Waking wearily, he gets up, lays down in bed, and quietly falls asleep, and slowly begins to dream ...

... as he slips back into the same nightmare, of walking down a dark foggy alley, past a couple of black guys shooting craps, who point to the corner. The worlds spinning as he turns the corner, and there is a very old black woman standing, leaning against a pole. She is not looking at Jack, but at something up the street. Jack turns, and looking through the fog, sees something lurking beside one of the massive, out of kilter library pillars.

Jack looks back to the old woman, to find himself looking up at a large shadowy demon, clothed in a purplish black peak hooded robe.

Jack is now holding a dying, bloody, little girl's limp body in his arms, her ripped open chest, exposing her heart, is pumping blood as the demon rips it out, and eats the throbbing child's heart. Then the demon raises its arm, and with a bloody skeletal finger extending out of the folds, turns and then points up to the library steps.

Jack turns and following the pointing finger sees the seductive leggy black girl, walking down the library steps, only now she is dressed like a prostitute instead. Jack tries to follow her, but she disappears into a sea of fog, he tries but cannot find her in the thick fog...

... As the fog starts to lift, he is walking down a dirt road, lined by dead, leafless trees, leading up on to a distant hill. He is carrying Nicole's Janie now, instead of the dead child's body.

As Jack walks along this dirt road, there is an old, ornate black Iron spiked fence, protecting a small abandoned weed strewn cemetery. Whose graves have disintegrating skeletal remains marking the graves instead of grave stones ...

At the end of the tree lined dirt road, as the fog seems to lift, we see off in the distance, an old, crumbling, gable roofed, mansion illuminated by the full moon lit sky ...

... Jack screams, as he realizes he is holding the bloody body of his little Nicole ...

... Awakening with a start, sweating profusely, staring wildly around the room, he is still partially dreaming, and he is in a panic. Then he realizes where he is, and starts to look for a drink in the darkened room ...

*   *   *

While Sheila sleeps undisturbed in her bedroom...

Nicole is also sleeping, but is awakened by scratching sounds, coming from the window. She gets up and

158

following the sound, looks out of her bedroom window. It is the big black cat from the cemetery, who is purring against the windows glass, looking in at Nicole.

Moments later Nicole is at an opened kitchen door, entering the house with the large black alley cat, slung over her little shoulder ... She carries the large black cat into her bedroom.

Happily sleeping now with her kitten, Nicole's holding her kitten as she sleeps. The black alley cat is lying beside her. Starting imperceptibly, her bed is beginning to lift slightly while she sleeps. When Sheila looks in on her little daughter, the black cat is gone. Sheila sits on Nicole's bed watching her little daughter, and later puts her head down beside Nicole and falls asleep.

Sheila awakens with an abrupt start as she feels something punching her in the back that seems to be coming from the bed itself. Her daughter Nicole is fast asleep and having another nightmare....

CHAPTER 29

The next morning Jack is back in the main Library at Logan Circle, sitting at a viewer, reading microfilm, scanning the … "New York Times---October 1877. Upstate New York Detectives, puzzled by strange ritualistic child murders. Decomposed little girls mutilated bodies found throughout park system, vital organs missing, crushed rib cages. No suspects arrested …"

Scrolling down through the articles, weeks, months, pass in a blur. "No new clues in children's murders, detectives baffled by horrific crimes."

Jack sits writing elements of the various articles, into his notebook.

        *   *   *

A slim delicate finger pushes a button, inset in the stone wall. The sound of a doorbell rings inside, then a young man opens the door, "Could I speak to a priest please," nervously fingering her wedding band.

"Follow me please, I'll see." The young man motions Sheila to enter the Rectory, and Sheila follows the young man down the steps, then hallway and into a small room on the right, "Please sit down, I'll see," he leaves.

Sheila waits apprehensively, wondering if she is doing the right thing, and as she stands up, and starts to leave. A kind voice is heard from behind her, startling her.

"Can I help you."

A deeply troubled Sheila seems to shake as she talks to the priest. "Please help me Father ..."

"Certainly my child." The older priest offers Sheila a chair by the desk, and then sits down himself. Looking at her kindly, "How can I help you."

"I, I don't know how to say this, I'm not Catholic or even, I'm not, I don't think, even religious ..."

The older priest watches her.

Sheila looks down, at the ground, at her feet ...

"It can't be that hard to say, can it?"

Sheila fidgets while looking down at the ground. … "I think my daughter is in danger," avoiding his eyes, "there's something unseen bothering her," crying uncontrollably, "please help me Father ..."

Extremely distraught, "Please help my daughter."

As the older priest watches her, a sadness over comes him.

*   *   *

Back at the Library, Jack sits at the viewer, continuing to read old microfilm ... "New York Times, October 1820—- New York City, child murders baffle police... missing disemboweled little girl's bodies found in Central Park..."

Jack stands at the library's reading room microfilm desk, he hands new requests to the girl behind the counter as he returns viewed microfilms ...

A despondent Jack unconsciously looks out of the window at the tree tops, and as he stands there, an unbearable sadness over comes him....

CHAPTER 30

Children are running around laughing, dozens of them, seemingly all over the place. As the music blasts, children are dancing, screaming with delight, as Nicole is opening presents laughing enchantingly.

Later Sheila is bringing in a large birthday cake with five burning candles, as Nicole is squealing with joy, and all the children are eating ice cream, cake, and hot dogs. Sheila's house is a mess, the laughter is intoxicating. Some of the children's parents are eating, while Sheila and Jack are bringing in drinks and more sandwiches.

Jack is helping Sheila in her kitchen.
        "Their all having a great time."
        Sheila is laughing, "I expect I'll be cleaning for a week." Nicole comes running in laughing. "Mommy, mommy thank you, thank you this is the best birthday party ever."
        Jack says, "Hi sweetie." Nicole hugs Jack affectionately, while Sheila smiles looking on.
        "I love you Uncle Jack," hugging her tightly.
"I love you too sweetie." Nicole happily runs back into the living room.

Later that afternoon Jack is leaving following Nicole's birthday party,
        "I may be back late tonight, if it's okay?"
        "Please, don't go Jack I'm scared to death about Nicole?"

Don't worry, I'll be back as soon as I can, don't worry Sheila."

"You promise? ..." Sheila reluctantly leaves and returns with a key, and handing it to him says. "We'll feel better if your here, Uncle Jack so come back, as soon you can okay? Please?"

Hugging her, "I'll be back tonight, don't worry." he kisses her on her cheek, and then he turns and leaves.

That night, little ghouls and monsters are all over the neighborhood walking with their parents as they are trick-or-treating. Carrying their candy filled bags from one house to the next.

At Sheila's house, her and her children are giving out candy to the little goblins, ghouls, and monsters. In the shadows of the many tall trees, something is watching the house from across the street.

Still later that evening, as Sheila is considering stopping handing out candy because of the late hour, a loud knocking is heard. Sheila opens the door, and a very large black robed demon looking trick-or-treater awaits its treat.

Sheila watches the demon, his face hidden from view, behind a lividly white skeletal face mask, and the purple black hood, and floor length monks robe. As nearly nakedly dressed young ladies are following behind him, at a discreet distance, following with a apparent reverence.

As he steps back, and with a nod of his robe covered head, the extremely sexy, nearly naked, masked and costumed young ladies with him, accept the candy offered by Sheila's children with a strangely evil smile. And then the demon who hasn't accepted anything, turns and bids his ladies to depart. As he leads them back out into the street again, his back turned to Sheila, his yellow eyes burn brightly beneath the robe's hood.

Sheila fearfully watches, as the oddly acting demonic looking trick-or-treater leaves, along with his entourage. A frightful Sheila quickly closes, and locks the front door. From the tree's shadows something is watching the house, as the front doors lights are turned off, to discourage any more trick or treaters. Moments later all the lights are turned off on the first floor, as other lights are turned on, on the second floor of the house.

Later Sheila is in Nicole's bedroom, putting a sleepy Nicole into her bed. Sheila covers her up, kisses her forehead, and hesitates before she exits the room, apprehensively watching as her daughter falls asleep.

As Nicole sleeps, out from under the bed, slithers the large black alley cat Nicole carried home from the graveyard the other day. It slinks over toward her feet, jumps onto the bed, and curls up beside her. As Nicole sleeps, the large black alley cats paw slowly changes into the ...

... gracefully shaped hand of the young black girl of Jack's nightmares. Gently caressing Nicole's hair, as she is lying curled up beside Nicole, purring like a cat, watching her as she sleeps. After a while the young black girl gets up out of bed, removes her black high heeled shoes, and tiptoes out of Nicole's bedroom. Down the hallway, opens the basement door and disappears down the steps into the dark basement.

Where she unlocks a casement window, and steps back as the window is being pushed open slowly....

... Powerful hairy hands are grasping the window sill, and something frightening is crawling through the window, head first, into the darkness of the basement ...

... With its powerful claw like hands clinging to the wall like a bat, as it crawls, head first, down the stone wall, and on to the basements concrete floor.

... From out of the darkness, at the basement floor, crawls out of antiquity, the demon, its yellow eyes glaring out from the darkness violently. The young black girl stands aside as it rises to its feet, and walks toward the steps. Smiling seductively, she licks her lips as she watches him approach. The demons powerful right hand caresses her long soft black hair as she is kneeling before him, then he walks past her and begins slowly climbing the steps, as she stands and follows him up the basement steps.

Walking on to the landing, through the door, and onto the hallway, she continues quietly following the demon down the hallway, passing Sheila's bedroom, past the other two girls bedrooms, to the door leading to Nicole's bedroom. The young black girl opens the door, for the demon, and it approaches a sleeping Nicole ...

... who suddenly bolts up, and screams a silent scream, her terrified eyes looking straight at the demon, but seeing nothing ... Nicole is dreaming ...

... Of seeing, as through a black fog, dead headless corpses walking around the bed. Their bodies are black and greenish brown; their clothes are rotting off of their decomposing bodies. Brown red clotted blood is leaking off their severed throats, as they walk around the bed. Mysterious chanting in an ancient archaic unknown language begins to be softly heard in the bedroom, its frightening melody adding to her terror.

Nicole's trying to scream but no sound is coming out ...

... As the purplish black peak robed demon, approaches her through the thick fog very slowly, its face unseen beneath the peaked robe, but for its brightly glowing yellow eyes, as it is approaching Nicole, while the headless corpses are continuing to circle her bed ...

... Awakening from her dream, Nicole is suddenly screaming, "Aaaaaahhhhhh help me ... help me, mommy ..."

Nicole is frightened out of her wits, while the sound of loud banging is heard, as the bed is rising up and down hitting the floor beneath her.

"Aaaaaaaahhhhhh, mommy help me, mommy, mommy ..."

... The banging sound, jars awake a sleeping Sheila, as she hears a screaming Nicole, she runs out of her bedroom, into the hallway. The banging's getting louder, as Sheila runs down the hallway to Nicole's bedroom, she pushes open the door as she enters, seeing Nicole sitting up in bed screaming uncontrollably. Sheila witnesses the entire bed lifting up into the air, and then banging back down on to the floor below, in pulsating gyrating movements ...

After watching in horror a few seconds, as the bed continues to lift up and down. She jumps onto the jumping bed to quiet her daughter's screaming, and with the bed going up and down with her on it, and holding a screaming Nicole, she slips pulling her daughter off of the bed with her, on to the floor. Looking under the bed, and seeing it is empty, as the bed lifts up in to the air and then crashes down again rhythmically on to the floor.

Standing up now, and backing out of the room, while holding a terrified Nicole in her arms, and shielding

169

her other two children who are cowering behind her, she exits the bedroom into the hallway, as the sound of the bed banging against the floor is deafening. Sheila watches momentarily, the bed lifting into the air higher, and higher as it bangs down, again, and again. Before Sheila races down the hallway, with her other children following their mother into her own bedroom. Slamming the door shut with a loud bang, and sound of the lock being turned, behind the closed bedroom door.

Sheila holds her children, shaking from fright, as they hear the sound of footsteps coming down the hallway. Moments later, they hear the quiet sound of the door knob being turned, watching it as it turns, first one way and then the other, something is turning the door knob. Suddenly someone or something is banging on the other side of the bedroom door, yelling on the other side of the door....

"Are you all right," now banging again on the door, "Sheila what's going on."

"Is that you Jack, Jack?"

"Yeah it's me, are you all right? Open up for God's sake."

Later that night, Jack is sleeping fitfully, on the sofa, murmuring under his breath, as he dreams ...

... Of being in near total darkness, beside a stairways wooden railings spindles ... looking through the spindles as a small child might, beneath the wooden hand railing, at the vast darkness below ...

... Where flickering candles illuminate the wooden staircase, winding lower, and lower, into the decaying mansions marble floored foyer below ...

... Suddenly crying out desperately, while being dragged, pulled by a giant hand, dragging him down the staircase, onto the dark foyer's cavernous marble floor.

170

Being dragged across the dark vastness, and through ornately carved wide double doors, on onto an adjoining dining room floor.

Where a long candelabra lit dining-room table, seemingly exquisitely arranged, impeccably decorated, diner awaits them, but a closer examination reveals ...

... In the flickering candle light, cobwebs clinging to the crystal chandelier, enshrouding everything, wine goblets, plates, and silverware. At the head of the table, in the dark is seated a shadowy figure, and seated along both sides of the table, a bevy of young beautiful women. Who are seemingly oblivious of the decay, eating voraciously, as blood is dripping from their mouths on to their evening gowns. While in the vast dark recesses, black hooded servants await their every desire. At the table, on a very large silver serving tray, a little girls blood soaked white dress, and the pieces of her gnawed, eaten, broken bloody skeletal remains can be seen ...

... As the meticulously dressed shadowy figure stands up, and looks at Jack, his blood splattered face still obscured in the flickering candle light...

... A terrified Jack bolts up, as he awakens with a terrified scream, and sits up, his eyes still seeing something moving in the dark ...

As the morning sun breaks through the clouds, it shines through Sheila's kitchen window, and we find her drinking a cup of coffee, while she is preparing breakfast.

Jack peeks into Nicole's bedroom, pausing at the door, Nicole's sleeping peacefully, holding her teddy bear

171

tightly to herself, Jack smile's a painfully sad smile, as he watches her sleep ...

Later Jack is seated at Sheila's kitchen table, while Sheila is cooking breakfast on the stove.

"I just wanted to let you know, that I'll be away for a day, maybe two."

"Today?"

"Yes," looking down apprehensively.

"But why, why now?"

"It's because of this," nervously twisting his wedding band, "this case I'm working on, I have to go to New York City, I'm meeting a famous psychiatrist lecturing at NYU. Who's going to help me understand Mythology, and its relationship to the criminal mind." Standing up and putting on his jacket, "He won't be there after today, I have to go."

"I'm scared," moving toward him, "please come back tonight, Uncle Jack okay?"

"Okay," Jack hugs her, "I'll be back tonight, for sure," hugs her tenderly, "don't worry?" Jack kisses her on the cheek, "I'll be back," and exits through the door.

"Thanks Jack." Sheila's quiet, deep in thought as she watches him leave.

CHAPTER 31

Captain Shaw sits at his desk, opposite Detective Thompson, deliberately avoiding his eyes. "Listen I put Detective Johnson, on to following Jack Ramsey days ago and ..."

A uniformed policeman interrupts Captain Shaw as he enters his office ...

"Shit, what the hell do you want?"

"Sir," handing him a piece of paper.

Captain Shaw reads the note just handed him, "When the hell did this happen?"

"His body was just found this morning, in an alleyway, beside a pile of trash."

"What the hell is going on around here, does anyone here know I work in this damn place?"

As he is leaving, "I wouldn't know Sir."

Captain Shaw hands Detective Thompson the sheet of paper. "Johnson's dead, found this morning, beaten to death, skull was crushed," looking around the room.

"I want this damned Jack Ramsey in irons, this afternoon ... understand me, Huh!"

Detective Thompson still reading, "I understand, but what makes you think Jack had anything ..."

Captain Shaw abruptly interrupts Detective Thompson.

"Because I say so," speaking fiercely, "So get a couple of officers and go the hell over to Jack's house, and lock his ass up," yelling, "understand me," to a retreating Detective Thompson, "and get the hell down to the damned morgue, and see if it really is Johnson."

*　　　　　　*　　　　　　*

Meanwhile Jack is driving down a small Manhattan side street, when a sudden thumping sound is heard, seconds before the steering wheel takes a sudden turn to the right, and the car lurches toward the curb. Jack pulls over and parks. Upon exiting the car, Jack discovers a flat tire. Jack looks despondently around, by the side of the car, before he opens the trunk and looks for the tire jack.

By the time Jack gets to the university's lecture hall, the lectures over, and from the back of the hall, as Jack enters, he can see the back of the head of a distinguished looking gentleman, talking to a few students. But before he can fight his way through the exiting student filled lecture hall, Jack watches hopelessly as Dr. Black exits from the front of the hall. Moments later exiting through the same door, a despondent Jack watches Dr. Black get into the back of a big black car, which then quickly speeds away.

*　　　　　　*　　　　　　*

At the same moment, near the front of a seemingly empty church, in one of the pews kneels a visibly shaken Sheila. Her head is down, her hands clasped together tightly resting against the back of the pew in front of her. As tears are running down her angelic face, her eyes down cast, she is silent, but sometimes mumbling quietly as she prays.

Watching her from within the darkness, at the rear of the church, beside a massive marble column, is someone or something that is casting a shadow upon the floor.

"Please dear God, please help my Nicole, help me and my children dear Lord."

As an almost indiscernible sound of footsteps, are approaching her from the rear of the church. Sheila is not aware of these sounds as she continues to pray quietly.

The shadow cast upon the floor is slowly approaching her very stealthily.

Sheila is unaware of the approaching shadow until it is almost upon her, only then does she react to the shadow on the floor hovering over her, she looks up to see ...

... The young man who was working in the church garden planting flowers, who gave her daughter a flower. He has a black sweat shirt over his other dark clothes.

"You scared me."

"I'm sorry, I didn't mean to scare you."

"I didn't hear you coming," a worried look brightens.

"I'm sorry, really," looking hopeful.

Sheila appears to be very uncomfortable, but then softens, smiling "Okay."

"Thanks," Mark, and Sheila laugh, then a guilty sadness, slowly over comes her again.

Later a visibly shaken Sheila, wanders into her living room, where Crosses are almost everywhere you look. She is straightening pictures of the Lord, and then kneels before a statue of the Blessed Virgin Mary, and praying beside her pictures. Which are also hanging all over the place, and on every table or flat surface.

CHAPTER 32

Under the cover of night an unmarked black police car sits, beneath a large tree, up the block facing Jack's house. Detective Thompson and another detective, who is behind the wheel of the vehicle, sit quietly watching the house. The detectives get out cautiously and approach the house, keeping in the shadows, close to the neighbor's shrubbery. Upon reaching Jack's lawn Detective Thompson puts his index finger to his lips, signaling the other detective to be quiet. Then they split up, as Detective Thompson motions for the other detective to go around to the back of the house. While Detective Thompson cautiously approaches Jack's front door.

At the front door, after expertly using a lock pick, he gains entry. Stealthily coming into the pitch black living room, and with the aid of a flashlight, he proceeds down the hallway, flashing the light into the bedrooms as he passes them.

Another unmarked police car pulls up unobtrusively across the street from Jack's house, and then numerous police cars also pull up in front of the house. The police exit their cars, some surround the building, and still others follow Detective Thomson through the front door into Jack's house.

Detective Thompson cautiously descends the basement's steps, holding a large blue black Glock automatic handgun. As Detective Thompson shines his flashlight in the dark, he sees lined up beside the far wall, dozens of earthen graves, dug through the concrete floor of the basement. And hanging on a nail, near the graves, is a blood stained, black hooded, long sleeved monks robe, a bright white mask of a skeletal face, and a pair of bloody rubber gloves which look remarkably like real hands. But are hairy and have long, claw like, sharp pointed bloody finger nails,

Later that night, policemen in white paper outfits, are digging up the graves, and stacking the innumerable bodies in rows along the other wall. Among the many other battered bloody bodies which weren't buried yet ...

... are Angela's bloody corpse and her daughter's half eaten body, along with a battered Charlie from the bar, and other acquaintances of Jacks....

        *   *   *

Two black over coated men are, knocking on Sheila's front door. As Sheila opens the door, she sees the older priest and Mark.

"Can we come in?"

"Of course Father," a smiling Sheila opens the door wider, "thank you so much," as they enter, and an awkward moment ensues.

"We came to bless this house, my dear, hopefully our presence may help you."

"Oh thank you Father, please come in, thank you," indicating the couch, "please sit down." The two men take off their top coats, revealing that Mark is also a priest.

Sheila looks surprised, and stares at Mark.

The older priest tries to console Sheila, "I understand that your daughter is having a problem."

"That's an extreme understatement Father, I saw and felt for myself the bed lifting and slamming down

180

onto the floor, while my … " trying not to cry, "daughter was screaming uncontrollably … " crying openly now, "she's terrified … there is something, some demonic possession here," pleading, "please help my daughter Father, please."

The priests look meaningfully, at each other.

Later Sheila's wiping away tears, beside the perking coffee pot, as Mark enters tentatively. Sheila doesn't hear him enter the kitchen.

"Ummmm," Father Mark walks closer, "the coffee smells good ..."

Looking down, avoiding his eyes, "I didn't think," softening, "I never thought you were," turning to him, "a priest."

Looking uncomfortable, "I know."

Father Mark begins to leave, but Sheila touches his sleeve, stopping his leaving. Just then Nicole runs into the room, "mommy can I help you?"

A smiling Sheila says, "Of course you can honey." Sheila carries the coffee into the living room, followed by Father Mark, and Nicole.

Later the older priest is blessing the house, sprinkling Holy Water around, mumbling a prayer in Latin.

CHAPTER 33

The next morning, back at the police station, swarms of seated uniformed police officers, swat teams, and detectives intensely listen attentively to Captain Shaw.

"Well, that's all I have to say about Detective Johnson, but he died doing his job, and now it's your turn to do your job." Looking around very forcefully.

"And, I want you to do your damn job, and get this son of a bitch arrested immediately, you hear that." Looking around angrily, "Now damn it, get the hell out of here, and get Jack Ramsey," screaming, "you hear me!"

*   *   *

Jack is holding open the door as Sheila and her daughter Nicole are entering the book store.

"I want a happy book Uncle Jack, a pretty book."

"You can get whatever you want Nicole, okay?"

"Thank you Uncle Jack."

"Your welcome honey."

The store is very crowded, and at the center of this large crowd, people are pushing to see the guest author. A distinguished gentleman, wearing a turban, is seated at a large table, behind numerous stacks of his book ...

... The book cover reads, "BEYOND INTUITION - THE FUTURE REVEALED," By Swami Mystic - Benin Shalayla.

Jack and Sheila politely make their way toward the crowd.

A turbaned aid says very humbly, "Please do not worry ladies, and gentleman, Mr. Shalayla, will sign everyone's copy of his book."

Interested in this Sheila comes closer, till she can almost see this Mr. Shalayla.

"Mommy, mommy I can't see."

Mr. Shalayla looks up from his book signing, and smiles graciously at the crowd, as Jack is picking up little Nicole, and putting her onto his shoulder.

As Mr. Shalayla scans the crowd, he seems to be suddenly troubled by something. He cannot take his eyes off of a smiling Sheila who standing beside Jack holding up a happy Nicole, so that she can see what's going on.

As Mr. Shalayla intently watches Sheila, he signals to the same turbaned aid who approaches him, and leans in closer. Mr. Shalayla whispers something into the turbaned aids ear, who then looks up directly at Sheila, who is watching animatedly. The author, Mr. Shalayla, continues to intently watch as, the turbaned aid makes his way around the crowd until he reaches Sheila. He leans into her, speaking politely.

"Excuse me Miss, Miss? ..."

Sheila turns, "Excuse me?"

"Pardon me Miss, but Mr. Shalayla desires to speak to you."

"Why?"

"This way please, Miss," indicating for her to follow, "this way please?"

An awkwardly surprised Sheila follows the turbaned aid through the crowd, as the people politely make way for them to pass. Jack follows as he squeezes in behind them, carrying a happy Nicole.

Upon their arrival at the table, Mr. Shalayla rises and stepping beside the table to Sheila, looks directly into Sheila's eyes. When he extends his hand to shake her hand, and touches her hand, he receives a kind of shock or jolt ...

... His eyes stare through her, seeing something else...

... he sees the hooded demon watching a young woman, walking in the woods beside a very young little girl ...

Sheila watches Mr. Shalayla intently.

... Mr. Shalayla sees the demon killing the young waitress, Angela in the park, as her child watches horrified ...

Sheila watches him, as the mystic shakes in spasms, while holding on tightly to her hand.

... He sees the demon eating Angela's little child's heart, as her blood soaks into the ground ...

"Please Miss, I'm very sorry to impose upon you in this way, but," looking straight at her, not seeing her ...

... But seeing the demon instead, as he talks, making Sheila very fearful as he talks to her ...

"I, uh, something is very wrong. You are in great danger ..."

... He not only sees the demon eating the young child's heart, but hears the sounds of crunching as the demon continues to eat the child's body, ravenously devouring flesh and bones alike, growling as it eats ...

'What do you mean?" Sheila tries to back away from the Swami, but he is still tightly holding onto her

185

hand. As Jack is listening quietly, but concerned as to what is going on.

… Mr. Shalayla is seeing the demon watching, through the iron bars of the playground's fencing, as Nicole's playing with her sisters on the merry-go-round ...

"Listen please believe me, I know it seems impossible, but believe me Miss I know all about you ...

"I don't understand."

Mr. Shalayla whispering, "Your little Nicole here, is in great danger."

"How do you know her name is Nicole," Sheila is deeply troubled, as she scrutinizes the Swami, listening to what he has to say.

Mr. Shalayla leans in closer, "You have had a terrifying experience, recently, but it's going to get much worse unless you listen to me." He again experiences a jolting spasm, "your other two daughters are in great danger too."

"How do you know that?" Shaking him, "Who are you?"

While a frightened Sheila heatedly talks to him, an oblivious Mr. Shalayla sees back in time, thousands of years to ...

... Ancient Sumerian desert sands, blowing wildly, forming towering knife edged mountains of sand. Standing in stark shadowed contrast, against the suns last dying embers of life, casting stunningly beautiful colored skies above the desert sands …

… As the extreme desert heat distorts the view, with its rising hot air, camels congregate beside an oasis, and interspaced beside the palm trees and cooling waters, sit ornately decorated enormous tents. And inside one of these ornate tents, on a deeply plush rug, in a very large lush opulently furnished tent ...

... Sits an old wrinkled looking demon, his large jewel ringed hand, reaches out in front of him, towards a three or four-year-old, extremely frightened, screaming little child of a girl ...

Mr. Shalayla is speaking to Sheila, but seeing these horrific visions instead, "Please forgive me, but your lives are in danger, Your IMMORTAL SOULS are in danger ..."

... The demon is seated now in front of a very young girl's lifeless body. Her little chest's been ripped apart ... her blood spreading out into a dark pool of blood, quickly moving out on to the rug ...

Mr. Shalayla, is still seeing into the past ... "This monster, this satanic demon devours children's souls. I know of what I preach. In India we know of these things to be facts."

As Mr. Shalayla speaks, he continues to see these visions ...

... Of the monster eating her pulsating heart ... Its bloody hands, holding the remnants of her pulsating heart ...

"Modern times causes people to disbelieve in anything that they cannot see or touch, but that does not mean that this is not so. It is a very powerful demon, of epic proportions, going back thousands of years."
A shaken Sheila stands transfixed unable to move away even though her eyes reveal a terror most intense, as she continues to try to free her hands from

his grip, and so also feels the jolting spasms Mr., Shalayla is also experiencing.

Mr. Shalayla experiences more jolting spasms, as he speaks to Sheila of ...

... Seeing an old abandoned cemetery, and the demon's powerful hands burying a stone Ossuary, into an open grave, while a little girl watches him thinking it is her dead bird ...

"You must go, and dig up what your grandfather buried, with your dead bird. Blood, finger nail clipping, hair he took from you, and put these beside his entombed ancient bones, in his stone Ossuary box, which he buried beneath your dead bird's small metal box..."

Mr. Shalayla himself is now terrified.

"The man you thought was your, grandfather wasn't your grandfather, the demon killed, and became him. You must dig up this stone Ossuary, from below the bird's metal box.

"And, destroy the cursed blood." Mr. Shalayla's hands are shaking with fear, as he looks around, "Please believe me," carefully watching the curious people lining up for the book signing, and leaning in to speak softly to Sheila. "Be exceedingly careful, you are all in extreme danger."

CHAPTER 34

Jack is sitting in Sheila's living room, holding a happy Nicole as she is looking through her birthday present, the book filled with animals of Africa, is obviously a big hit.

Jack notices something among the many pictures on the fireplaces mantel. Carrying Nicole in his arms until he reaches the picture, partially hidden behind the many other picture frames. Is a very old picture of a very young Sheila, perhaps two or three years old, standing with her mother, and an older man partially hidden from view. But behind them there in the distance, is an old dilapidated cemetery filled with very old statues, angels, and Crosses, many of which are broken lying on the ground.

It is the cemetery of Jack's nightmares, viewed from the dirt road. Jack picks up the picture, spellbound … suddenly hearing the sound of footsteps behind him, Jack spins around, and sees it is Sheila standing behind him.

"Oh, you scared me ... I'm sorry, I guess I'm just jumpy."

"I'm sorry I scared you." Sheila watches, as Jack goes back to looking at the picture in his hands ...

"It's my mother, and my grandfather."

Jack is pointing to the cemetery in the picture.

"But the place."

"The place?" Looking at the picture, "Oh, that's my grandfather's family cemetery plot. The old house is up on the hill."

"The cemetery," indicating the picture, "it's in my nightmares." A frightened Sheila, and Jack look at each other, afraid to think what this might mean.

Later Sheila is at Audrey's front door, while her two older daughters, are standing behind Audrey. Sheila suddenly hugs Audrey.

"Thanks loads Audrey," now hugging her daughters, "now you girls be good, you mind Audrey, and I'll be back late tonight," turning as she is leaving, "bye girls."

Sheila is busily locking up her house, while Jack is helping Nicole into his car, when the young priest, Father Mark approaches her house. Father Mark has a very serious look as he approaches her.

"I'm sorry I should have called." She hastily puts her keys away.

"No, it's all right," walking away towards the car, as she speaks, "it's just that I'm late." Looking off to Jack, "look we're leaving now and," starting to cry, "I'm sorry it's just I'm so worried."

Grasping her gently, "But, where are you going," trying to stop her from leaving, "maybe I could help?"

"Father," hesitating, as she is looking around uncomfortably, "I feel funny, calling you Father," hurrying away, "you can't, help, nobody can help."

"What's wrong?"

Sheila walks to the car, and gets inside closing the door. As Father Mark follows her.

"But I want to help." Jack unlocks the door, and motions for him to get inside.

Getting into the back seat of the car.

"Thanks," looking at Jack, and then to Sheila, as he speaks, "I want to go with you."

Sheila looks at Father Mark apprehensively.

CHAPTER 35

A somber looking Jack is driving along a darkening, narrow, winding tree lined road. Beside him sits Sheila, who is holding a sleeping Nicole, and in the back seat Father Mark.

Their cars traveling very fast, as it slows beside a small dirt road, Jack's car turns onto the smaller road. His headlights illuminate this dark, narrow, tree lined dirt road, as it snakes its way through the woods. A fast approaching break in the tree line on the right reveals a black iron estate fenced, very old cemetery in extremely deteriorated condition, and up on a distant hill sits an old gable roofed mansion.

Jack's black car drives through an opened gate, into the cemetery, continues along the grassy path beside the woods, over a small hill, and disappears amid a grove of extremely thick pine trees.

From out of the wooded darkness, Sheila emerges flashlight in hand leading them, out of the grove of trees, and onto the moonlight lit small path, through the rough, high weed filled lawn leading back into the cemetery. As the looming moss covered tombstone statues, tower over the walkway.

Walking between rows of giant crack weathered angels, whose out stretched wings cast long moonlight lit shadows across the graves. Standing beside ancient deteriorating Crosses of all description, parts of which lay deliberately broken upon the weed filled ground.

Sheila slows to catch her bearings, and then walks toward the largest old tree. She then looks around slowly closing her eyes, every so often, while continuing to turn around slowly, holding Nicole's hand ever so gently.

Glancing up at the large tree which towers above her, leaning against it, then sliding down to a crouch, she feels with closed eyes, feeling up along the tree to a spot where an old broken iron spike extends from the bark. Fingering it she then opens her eyes, and then looking down at a particular spot, near the tree's base, where a cruelly broken tombstone, covered in weeds lies.

"I remember this place, my grandfather took me here one rainy day, supposedly to bury my dead bird. We buried it but," slowly, deliberately, "he also buried something else."

Looking around hesitatingly, and then more decidedly she kneels down, looks to Jack, and nods to a spot beside the stone, pointing with her finger ...

"It's here, it's buried here."

Father Mark starts to walk back toward to car.

"I'll get the shovels, and a flashlight."

Nicole's playing around the tomb stones, picking wild flowers ...

Later, Jack and Father Mark are taking turns swinging the pickaxe into the earth, wiping the sweat from their faces, and then later taking turns with the shovel, lifting the dirt out carefully. Then back to swinging the pickaxe again, and then again taking turns shoveling lifting out the dirt.

196

Jack thinks he has hit something, kneeling down, and digging now with his fingers, he slowly uncovers something, it is an old rusted metal cash box ...

Jack reaches down, picks it up, and lifts the lid, inside is a dead bird's skeleton.

Jack looks up at Sheila, and putting the bird's box down, continues to dig, slowly at first, and then later with more enthusiasm until, the shovel again has hit something solid.

Father Mark motioning toward Nicole, "Maybe I should take Nicole for a little walk back to the car, I'll wait there for you."

"Thanks, but you'd better take the flashlight with you" Sheila kisses her Nicole, and tells her to, "run along with Father Mark honey."

Laughing happily, Nicole says, "Okay mommy." Jack watches as they walk off slowly, and then resumes digging until he finds it. At first it just looks like an oblong stone, but Jack keeps digging.

As Jack lifts it out of the hole in the ground ... It becomes apparent that it is an ancient, solid hand hewn stone Ossuary box. One-foot-high, one-foot-wide, and two feet long, with a wax sealed stone lid. And chiseled into the stone, is something in an ancient language.

The anciently designed Archaic Seal is still intact, same design as on the demon's ornately jeweled ring, and Jack and Sheila look at each other not knowing what to do now ...

They cut through the seal, take off the heavy stone lid, and looking inside, they find an ancient, decaying linen cloth, enwrapping something the size of a baby. But it's getting too dark to see anything, so they decide to walk back to the car, leaving the now barely visible birds grave behind.

Walking back through the tree canopied cemetery, weaving their way between the cracked, broken, and toppled grave stones. A weary Sheila walks beside Jack who is carrying the now closed stone Ossuary box.

As the moon eerily lights their way back through the weed filled path, heading toward the grove of thick pine trees, where Jack parked his car. Sheila follows a few feet behind, and searches the area about her, looking more, and more concerned.

Upon reaching the grove of thick wooded trees, the black cars open doors look suspiciously vacant ...

Sheila nervously looks for her daughter, looking about for her in the darkness.

"Jack," Sheila's running now, "where are they? Where is Nicole and Mark?"

Cautioning Sheila to be quiet, and not to move, he stealthily moves toward the car, gun in hand. A very concerned Jack looks nervously into the car, as he whispers out ...

"Oh my God ..." Dropping the Ossuary box, turning, and hurrying back to stop Sheila from coming any closer, before she could get to the car, and see anything inside.

"Shhh," whispering, "don't make a sound, you might endanger Nicole." Jack stops her from approaching any further.

On the car's rear door, and seat, is massive amounts of blood, trailing on to the ground, where a large pool of blackening blood lies, and beside the pool of blood, blood stained smears on the matted grass, distanced apart, like someone's bloody foot prints.

Leaving a crying terrified Sheila, Jack walks back and kneeling down, examines the blood evidence. He touches a portion of the blood drops, and rubs his fingers together, the blood is dry.

Sheila tries to scream, but only a frightened whisper is heard, "Jack."

Suddenly Sheila signals Jack to where she is standing, pointing to something at the base of her foot ...

... A small trail of blood, and a two-foot-wide path of flattened tall grass, leading into the woods. And beside the bloody trail, are those blood stained foot prints on the grass.

Sheila is trying not to cry, as Jack retrieves a flashlight from the car's trunk. Then shines the flashlights beam onto the pool of blood, and then back to the trail of blood at Sheila's feet. Following the trail of blood leads them to a very thick area of bushes, where they find another very large pool of black clotting blood, and hidden in the brush ...

...The flashlight illuminates Mark's lifeless body, lying there beaten horrifically to death, bloody chest ripped apart, his heart missing, but there is no sign of Nicole, as Sheila is crying, quietly shaking uncontrollably.

Jack kneels beside Father Mark's body, and feels his neck, "He's been dead at least an hour."

Uncomprehendingly, "What do you mean," looking back to Father Mark's body, "we were just with him."

Jack is now examining the soles of Marks shoes, there is no sign of blood. "No, whatever we were with, it wasn't Father Mark."

She is terrified, "But ... he was with Nicole?"

Jack takes her hand, "Let's go."

Shining his flashlight beam onto the bloody foot prints, which lead away from the priest's body. They begin to follow the blood stained foot prints path ...

... The path leads them back, beneath the pale moonlight lit cemetery, walking in and out of the shadows cast upon the ground, by the towering stone statues, and broken Crosses. They come to a break in the fence, leading back, and out onto the dirt road. They walk through this break in the fence, onto the dirt road.

Jack looks through the iron spiked estate fencing, at the darkened tombstone's towering shapes, and then to the road ahead, at the dark old mansion on the top of the hill ...

..."It dawned on me, as we walked, that this was in my dream, my nightmares. But as I walked along this dirt road, approaching the deteriorating mansion up on the hill. I suddenly realized that I had been here before, and feared what awaits us ..."

... Jack stares ahead, and trembles quietly, almost imperceptibly. Ahead on the hill, the dark abandoned, deteriorating mansion sits impassive, resolute.

Then suddenly a faint candle light is seen moving along the first floor's row of windows ...

... slowly from one window to the next. An angrily determined Jack and Sheila look at each other ...

Jack and Sheila are much closer now, as they move secretively toward the dark mansion. Upon reaching the end of tree cover, the dusty road leads right up to and ends in a circle at the mansions front doors.

They duck into the thick shrubbery surrounding the mansion, and crawl along toward the front door ...

Whispering to Sheila, while peering into the darkness surrounding them, "Wait for me here."

"Why can't I come with you?

"What if I don't come back, who will go for the police? Now here's the keys to the car."

Reluctantly giving up.

"All right, but be careful."

Standing up in the shadows, but still hidden from view of the house. Jack kisses Sheila on her cheek, and then exits the darkness of the shrubbery, and approaches the dark decaying mansion, looking apprehensively around as he does.

He proceeds to the front door, and attempts to pick the lock with a lock pick, but while holding the doorknob, it turns and the door opens, with a creaking sound.

… Pausing momentarily, Jack takes out his blue black Glock automatic and enters into the pitch black mansion …

Jack's flashlight beam illuminates a small circle, in the blackened foyer, as he stealthily crosses the vast empty space. Jack shines the flashlight beam around the walls and ceilings. It reveals a wide staircase leading up into a pitch black landing, and a very large stained glass window of unusual design looming over it. The wide stairway ends on the hallways landing at the base of the stained glass window, but it then continues up both sides of the walls into a vast arching ceiling, disappearing into the darkness above. The flashlights beam follows the landing, and exposes a circular banister running around the entire second floor.

Watching through the spindles of the banister, we see Jack is investigating the interior of the mansion's pitch black foyer, his flash light beam moving about in the darkness below … As the sound of the front door creaking open alarms Jack, and he looks for someplace to hide …

… Someone is entering the house cautiously, Jack puts out his flashlight quickly, and backing up against the wall, he is intently watching the opening door, as a dark shadow enters.

A whispered, "Jack," is heard.

The flashlight's beam of light illuminates the floor again.

Jack whispers, "Over here."

201

"I was afraid for you coming in here alone," clutching at his arm, and looking around, "and I didn't want to be alone either."

"Okay."

Gesturing for Sheila to follow him, as he walks cautiously on to, and over an extremely large, blood red colored, mosaic pentagram, his flash light's beam has illuminated on the floor of the pitch black mansion.

They continue walking in the dark, over to a large pair of tall wide, very ornately designed, demonically carved wooden doors, he has discovered to their right. Apprehensively opening one of these doors, and entering as Sheila is following in behind him.

Jack's flashlight beam illuminates a small circle of light in the large bookcase lined room. As Jack is walking around in the dark, his shadowy form is blocking Sheila's view of some of the rows of books on the one wall.

Sheila uses her cigarette lighters flame now, while moving about in the dark at the other end of the room.

In the darkness of the stairwell, looking down through the cob web filled wooden spindles of the banister, at the faint flickering light coming out of the opened library's doorway. A whispered voice is heard, echoing out of the library's opened doors into the shadows.

"There's dust everywhere Jack."

"Let's get out of here."

"Okay."

A flickering illusion of light is being cast onto the vast darkened foyer below. Illuminated by Sheila's cigarette lighters flame as they are exiting the library, followed by their shadowy faces, entering into the darkness of the foyer ...

As Jack's flashlight casts a small circular beam of light, pinpointing into the intricate vastness, and then on toward the large pair of door's on the opposite side of the foyer ...

... Watching them from between the wooden spindles, as they are walking across the foyer's vast floor below, and then walking through the large doors ...

… As they enter the vast darkness, Jack's flashlights beam is searching out the elegant dining room, its table set as for a sophisticated dinner party. The crystal goblets, plates, silverware immaculately set, but a closer inspection reveals it covered in cobwebs, dropping from the candle sticks, and cobweb filled low hanging candelabra. After making a cursory examination, Jack and Sheila make a hasty exit out through the doorway.

As the shadowy pair are following their small circle of light back onto the pitch black foyer, they walk to, and then hesitate at the stairwell's steps, looking apprehensively up into the darkness.

Watching them through the spindles of an upper stairwells banister, they are now climbing the steps, up into the wide rising staircase....

Upon reaching the second floor, and on to the, extremely wide, hallway which continues off in both directions. Jack and Sheila find themselves beneath the extremely large, ornately designed, colorful pentagram, depicted within a massive stained glass window. Whose moonlight lit colors spring to life in the darkness of the night.

Torn between which way to go, they decide to continue going on up one of the two extremely dark staircases. Looking about them as they climb the spiraling staircases assent up into the upper floors.

... Halfway up the staircase ... Sheila whispers.

... "Wait," as she is straining to hear.

... They hear something very softly, almost indiscernible...

... it's a child crying ...

... "That's Nicole," unable to speak, then. "That's my child," but they don't know which way to go, because the faint crying seems to be echoing from different directions ...

Sheila choking back tears, "Where is she?" ...

Jack motions her to be quiet, and then tries to listen from different directions on the stairway ...

Signaling for her to stay where she is, a resolute and determined Jack is furtively climbing the remaining steps, gun in hand, searching into the darkness ...

As a terribly frightened Sheila stands below in darkness, except for her cigarette lighter's yellow flickering flame …

While above on yet another flight of steps, from behind a wooden banister, between wooden spindles. Bright yellows eyes are peering down onto Jack, who is standing in the dark, listening in total silence ...

As Jack is straining to hear, he thinks he hears the child's crying is coming from somewhere far below.

…but from somewhere above, Jack hears something coming down the steps ...

… While in the darkness of the stairway, as Sheila is standing holding a flickering yellow flame, looking up past Jack …

… she sees a dark shadowy shape seemingly flying down the steps ...

... Out of the darkness a red yellow flame flares, and a gunshot rings out, Crack, followed by Crack, Crack, Crack.

As a terrified Sheila rushes up into the darkness of the upper steps, a frightened Jack is rushing back down, "I shot something up there, it wasn't human. Nicole's not up there," pulling her as he is rushing down the steps, into the lower depths of the ancient decaying mansion.

While running down the steps, they both hear footsteps closely following them, racing down the steps.

"She's in the basement."

Upon reaching the foyers main floor, Jack turns as he hears clawed footsteps behind him. Looking up he sees three sets of yellow eyes racing down at them. As the sounds of growls, and loud snarling, are also now heard, followed by the sound of them racing down the steps from above.

Jack turns, pulling Sheila onto one of the long hallways jutting off in either direction. Running down the hallway off to their left, they hear something quickly gaining on them. Looking back, they see very large, yellow eyed, black dogs, turning onto the hallway, and gaining on them quickly.

Jack opens a door on their left, it is a closet. Looking back, the voracious dogs are almost upon them. Sheila tries to open the door next to the closet, it opens. Jack and Sheila hurry through the doorway, just as the voracious black dogs are on to them, the sound of them banging into the opened door is heard before it closes. Then the sounds of scratching, and loud growling, on the other side of the door.

But as Jack slams the door closed behind him, he loses his grip on the flashlight, and it falls down the steps, its light bouncing down into the void below, and then the light goes out, Jack whispers ...

"Shit."

In the darkness nothing can be seen, then a small flame flares up, as Sheila's shadowed face is seen looking toward the echoing sound of a crying child, which can be heard much louder now.

"Jack, where is she?"

"I don't know," forcefully, "but I know she's here."

As Sheila continues to hold the lit cigarette lighter, its flickering flame exposes Jack's gun, glinting blue black, as he disappears into the depths of the stairway below. Following him, Sheila slowly disappears, as her lighter's flickering flame's light goes out plunging them both into total darkness again.

Jack's shadow is groping around, on all fours feeling around in the dark for his flash light.

"That's my foot."

"Oh sorry ..."

As Sheila's lighter flares up again, illuminating a small area in the basement.

Then a slight breeze, blowing through, plunges them back into total darkness, as the flame goes out.

"I couldn't continue to hold it, wait," as the flame flares up again, out of the darkness ...

... a very week voice is heard, in the dark, extremely close by ...

Suddenly the flames light flutters in the darkness, then their almost thrown back into total darkness, but the flame flares up again ...

Jack whispers, "Listen," a faint sound is heard ... a very weak. "Mommy, please help me mommy," Jack is feeling along the floor of the damp basement with his fingers, and he finds a door way. Jack begins banging against the door, almost imperceptibly ...

... "Help me," is heard.

206

Jack breaks the door down, and bursts into a cramped tiny stone walled cell, and there tied up on a dirty bed, is a crying Nicole. Sheila breaking down crying out …

… "Oh my baby, please forgive me." Nicole's almost catatonic, seeing and yet not knowing.

As Sheila carries a crying Nicole out of the dirty cell, a sudden breeze extinguishes the cigarette lighters flame, again thrusting them all back into the total darkness.

"Feel that Sheila, a breeze," while out of the darkness of the dirty basement, a squeaking sound is heard.

"Jack."

"What?" The cigarette lighters flame flares up again illuminating Sheila's face.

"There's something over there."

"What?"

Sheila is holding out the cigarette lighters flickering yellow flame.

"There …"

… There is something in the darkness, piled up along the wall, stacks of balls or something …

"Oh my God …"

"What," Sheila's hand moves the flame's light closer to the wall …

… It is little children's skulls, little mummified children's skulls, and behind their skulls, their skeletal remains …

Stacked from the floor, high into the ceiling, one upon the other along the wall, disappearing into the darkness as far as the eye can see in either direction.

"It's bodies …"

Sheila, "Aaahhh, oh my god …"

Jack moves closer, examining the bodies…

"They could be hundreds of years old …"

Cobwebs are everywhere, honey combing the mummified children's bodies, dust several inches' thick cover them, as rats are rummaging loudly among the little bodies. The light has apparently frightened the numerous rats, the sounds of their squeaking is now loudly heard, as the flame's light is again fluttering ...

... Jack takes Sheila's cigarette lighter, and darkness is again thrust upon them, as the flame blows out. Jack holds the lighter in the darkness.

"We're in a bad way here, let's go toward the source of the breeze." Reigniting the lighters flame again.

"Okay," looking back at the steps.

"But let's hurry," handing Sheila the lighter as the flame goes out, and taking the little child into his arms.

The cigarette lighters flame flares up again, and illuminates the darkness slightly, held out by Sheila's hand, jutting into the dark.

Jack is carrying Nicole and pointing his Glock automatic, as he moves into the uncertainty ahead. The lighters flame illuminating squealing rats, scurrying over the children's skeletal remains, stacked along both sides of the walls, as they inch their way through the ever narrowing basements tunnel.

Off in the distance a very faint light can be seen, as the sounds of the ferocious dogs can still be faintly heard off in the distance behind them.

Now hurrying as fast as they can in the darkness....

... they run up against an old rusted, thick iron spiked gate, blocking their way out of this hell hole. Jack hands Sheila back, her unconscious Nicole.

In the light of the flickering flame, she is holding Nicole, while Jack is trying to move the iron gate, dislodge it from its frame, but he cannot budge it, it is locked.

"Jack, how are we going to get out of here."

He tries again to dislodge the gate from its frame, this time much more forcefully. Giving up he takes out a small case from his inner jacket pocket. Jack removes one of the lock picks.

"I don't know, we may have to go back the way we came, but I'm afraid of what's there now." Jack's hands shake, as he tries to pick the lock.

Suddenly the sounds of the barking dogs are much louder,

"Someone, or something must have opened the basement door."

In a terrified voice, "Jack, can you get it?"

"I don't know?"

The moon's eerie light, suddenly illuminates the cemetery's tombstones, which lie beyond the iron bars, off in the distance.

"Jack can you get it open."

"I don't know," Jack's hands shake, dropping the lock pick. Grouping around in the dark he cannot find it.

"What do we do now Jack?"

"I don't know, wait." Jack kneels down onto the stone floor at the base of the iron gate. He is trying to pry up one of the stones, at the base of the gate, with his fingers, but he is not having any success.

Suddenly the sounds of the barking dogs are much closer ...

Moving on to another one of the stones, he nervously succeeds in dislodging one of the stones, it is long and narrow but thick, and looks heavy ...

Jack's shaking hands lifts it, and sticks the stone in between the iron spiked gate, and the stone wall. Prying with the stone, he is straining to bend or break the gates hinge. He cannot budge it ...

The sounds of the viciously barking dogs are even closer now ...

Sheila lends a hand, and as the two of them strain against the stone, the iron bars seem to be moving....

The approaching loud sounds of the barking dogs indicate their imminent appearance seem only moments away now ...

Straining to see into the darkness of the long tunnel behind them, seems to reveal that somethings coming at them, and fast ...

... Then all at once, the iron bars bend...

... The openings small, but first Sheila squeezes through the small opening of the iron bars, then Jack hands Sheila an unconscious Nicole, and then Jack squeezes through just as the voracious, extremely large black dogs are now upon them, growling and snarling maniacally, trying to get through the gaps in the bars.

Jack fires his gun into the dogs until he has no more shells ...

As they turn to run, they find themselves back in the old cemetery, when ...

...Out of the darkness the demon viciously springs upon Jack, as Jack exclaims ...

... "Run Sheila, Run" ...

Sheila hesitates for a second, then while still holding her daughter Nicole, she runs off into the night ...

... While Jack, and the demon are locked in a vicious struggle

Later police car's lights are flashing everywhere, as an unconscious hand cuffed bloody Jack, is being shaken awake …

… Jack's coming to now, and looking around, as detectives, and uniformed police officers are looking down at the dead priest's horrifically bloody, dismembered body, lying in a large pool of blood.

Later Jack is being led away, hand cuffed behind him, as he cries out.

"No, for God's sake, it's him, not me, don't you see."

Just then a big burly policeman steps forward and punches Jack in the mouth, knocking him to the ground, and then kicking Jack in the mouth, until he is unconscious.

The police are now dragging an unconscious Jack by his feet, face down, along the ground heading toward an awaiting police van.

CHAPTER 36

Back on the physiatrist couch, a drugged Jack awakens to realize that he has been talking to the psychiatrist ... Looking around the room Jack seems dazed, as he looks toward the sound of Dr. Black's voice.

"You've had a powerful injection of a truth serum Jack, and I've been listening to your interesting story. Let me get Nurse Johnson in here."

A fussy headed Jack, because his head is almost now hanging off the couch, watches Dr. Black's feet walk to his desk, as the Doctor is leaning forward over the desk, his fingers pushing a button on an intercom.

"Nurse Johnson, please bring in another injection for Mr. Ramsey, thank you."

Sounding very sexy, almost like a purring moan.
"Yes Doctor Black."

Jack watches the doorways floor as the door opens, and the nurses sexy bright red high heeled shoes enter the room. At her waist concealing the rest of her, is the bottom of a shiny stainless steel tray.

Jack turns to Dr. Black, whose back is still turned to him as he writes something into an opened notebook on the desk.

Jack's blood shot, blackened eyes reveal he is exhausted, and is seemingly feeling hopeless in his distress.

The stainless steel tray, upon which lies a seemingly very large needle and a small bottle of some brown looking unknown substance, is being carried into the room, by the unseen nurse's, sharp pointed, bright red finger hailed looking hands.

Jack's eyes are following her hands as they are lifting the large needle from the tray.

Nurse Johnson's eyes are intently watching Jack, from behind a surgical mask which is covering the rest of her lower face.

She is extracting a brown liquid from the small bottle, filling the large needle to the brim.

Jack is watching quietly as she wipes his forearm with a small cotton swab, and as she is preparing to inject his arm with the needle full of the brownish liquid. Jack quickly tries to get up, so that she cannot inject him with the needle ...

... But suddenly an extremely powerful, big ringed, hand block his escape, holding Jack to the couch effortlessly.

As the needle point pricks Jack's forearm, and its brown contents is plunged into his veins ...

Jack's eyes wince as the liquid fill his veins ...

A look at the small, now empty, bottle's label reveals its brown liquid contents to be Heroin.

Nurse Johnson's fingers have finished emptying the Heroin filled needle into Jack's veins. As she removes it, she swipes his arm with a cotton swab, and places a band aid, on the puncture wound.

The Heroin's rushing into Jack's blood stream, and Jack's head is spinning, as he leans back against the couches pillowed armrest ... his blurred vision of the room, seems to be spinning around in circles.

While Nurse Johnson's eyes, above her surgical mask, watches Jack with a cruel interest.

Jack's blurred vision is still spinning around in circles, as Nurse Johnson's face mask is pulled down slowly revealing her face ...

214

... Nurse Johnson, is revealed to actually be Jack's missing wife Diane, but she is much, much younger, a young girl really but it is still her, and she is smiling, cruelly.

Later inside padded cell number #-22, a somber, disheveled, weary Jack, walks back and forth between the narrow walls, mumbling incoherently as he walks ...

... suddenly he stops, and looks up ...

... Jack's tear filled, black socketed, blood shot eyes stare wildly up into the prison cells concrete ceiling....

... falling to his knees, "Don't you understand Lord," begging ...

"... It's him, help me, help me please, help me please," his eyes close while crying out, "please give me a chance to defeat him, a second chance. A second chance to save Sheila, and her children, please."

... Staring into the ceiling, "They don't understand, he'll kill them, I know now who he is ..."

"... I can't live with this on my soul ..."

Crying now uncontrollably as he screams, "Please help me, help me ... or please kill me."

CHAPTER 37

Black clouds are looming above the sky, as the setting sun casts its bright red, and yellow dying embers, above this seemingly endless tree lined road. A break in the trees reveals, a quickly setting sun, as falls last vestige of dying leaves are gusting into the air, at increasingly strong intervals as the impending storm fast approaches.

The black limousine slows at a gated entrance fast approaching on the right. As an old, and weathered bronze sign, blowing back and forth in the wind, at the entrance reveals, the "Northeastern Pennsylvania Asylum for the Criminally Insane."

Its gated entrance bars the way, but the policeman in the guard house, recognizing the black car, opens the gates on to the prison hospital's wooded grounds. Driving along the tree lined road, leading to the asylum, as its magnificent stone structure's decaying edifice fills the distant horizon.

Silently watching through the grimy multi-paned glass, of a large old wooden window, as the approaching black limousine drives up to the entrance to the asylum, and parks beyond the lawn, out on the driveway's circular cul-de-sac.

The wide exterior entrance door of the hospital opens, to reveal the big black car out on the front lawn. We watch the back of Dr. Black, and the now young Diane beside him, as they are seen walking arm in arm, toward the big black car's rear door.

The rear door opens, and inside the limousine we see the young black girl of Jacks nightmares, is sitting quietly, and seductively smiling back as they enter the car.

We see Dr. Black's view of the young black girl as he is getting into the car, Jack's Diane follows Dr. Black into the car ...

... The young black girl, is watching the back of the well dressed, distinguished looking Dr. Black looking back toward the asylum, while his large powerful hand, wearing the large unusually designed ring, slowly slips down onto Diane's black stockinged legs ...

... Then taps on the glass, separating the limousine from the driver ...

... The glass lowers and in the rear view mirror is seen the driver, who looks like a dead man, looking back, the driver calmly adjusts the rear view mirror ...

... Till he sees in the mirror, the distinguished well-dressed Dr. Black's face ...

... It is a distorted, blurry, foggy livid, dead white skeletal face, as if it is a mask ...

... Its skeletal teeth seem to protrude well away from its blurry face ...

... Several inches from its blurry face ...

... Its yellow eyes burning into your soul ...

... Its skeletal teeth opening in a deep throaty laugh.

"Drive home."

The dead looking driver's looking into the rear view mirror, as he responds in a dead like answer, "Yes sir."

... in the rear view mirror, the driver sees the demon looking back toward the asylum, as the one-way mirror glass begins sliding closed, blocking off the view into the back seat as it goes up ...

The cars moving quickly now, as the asylum fades away into the distance ...

... The demon is looking back, at the fast fading asylum, but a look at the back of his head, reveals that behind the demon's right ear, and between the hair ...

... The black colored numbers 666 are clearly seen ...

... As his hand rubs the black stockinged leg of the now young Diane, at his side, and at her feet an unconscious nearly naked Sheila, who is bounded with her hands tied....

... and beside her an unconscious Nicole, who is dressed up like a little prostitute...

... but her lip stick has been smeared, her clothing torn and ripped ...

As the black girl seductively asks, "How's Jack, is he okay?"

... An evil looking Diane is smiling cruelly, seated next to an even more evil smiling ...

... Much younger, looking Jack ...

... or?

... Someone who looks like Jack, who says....

... "He's fine," cruelly, "my son is fine."

THE END

Ronald Haak is an actor, who had portrayed Mayor Silkowski opposite a sterling JASON MILLER. In Mr. Miller's, 'Tour de force,' portrayal as Coach, in Jason's world famous "PULITZER PRIZE," winning play:
    ... "THAT CHAMPIONSHIP SEASON." ...
Performed in Scranton, and in the Rittenhouse Square area of Philadelphia, Pennsylvania. Ron also appeared with Mr. Miller in "Inherit The Wind," and in "The Cane Mutiny," for Scranton Public Theatre, in Philadelphia City Hall's Courtroom #253.

    Ron also directed a stellar JASON MILLER, in Jason's outstanding play:
    ... "BARRYMORE'S GHOST" ...
In which Jason Miller's portrayal of the tumultuous life of the late John Barrymore, overwhelmed the audiences, successfully receiving standing ovations, night after night, by the enthusiastically crowded audiences in Philadelphia, Pennsylvania. But sadly this was Mr. Miller's last season of 'Tour de force' performances on the stage, as he passed away, all too soon afterwards.

Ron also had directed his brother Richard Haak, in Eugene O'Neill's award winning play, "Hughie," in Philadelphia and New York City. Jason Miller who saw Rick's performance, said: ... "It was the finest portrayal of Erie Smith I had ever witnessed, on broadway or off. A very powerful 'Tour de force' performance, unmatched by even the famous actors that I knew well."

Some of Ron's stage credits include:
Pale in "Burn This," Teach in "American Buffalo,"
The VP in "Thank You Madam President," Richard
Henry Lee in "1776," Inspector William Hopkinson
in "The Kamagata Maru Incident," Tilden in "Buried
Child," and Gately in "Private Wars." Ron is also a
member of SAG/AFTRA and EQUITY.

Ron studied acting for almost ten years at
the Wilma Theatre, with the acclaimed acting
teacher, Gordon Phillips. Who had earlier taught in
New York City, at the renowned "Actors Studio,"
with the world famous, "Lee Strasberg."

His other acting teachers included, Mike
Lemon a prominent Philadelphia casting director,
and acting teacher. He also studied acting at "The
Wilma Theatre," with both its original founders,
creative artists, and directors Blanka & Jiri Zizka.

Ron also studied with the famous actor
George DiCenzo. Who was a director, producer,
scene study coach and renowned acting teacher in
Los Angeles, New York City, and Philadelphia.

George DiCenzo, who played a detective in the
movie, THE EXORCIST III said of this story: ...

**"IT IS UNDOUBTEDLY THE SCARIEST
SCRIPT I HAVE EVER READ."**

Made in the USA
Middletown, DE
09 August 2017